A CLOSE BRUSH
WITH LIFE

A CLOSE BRUSH WITH LIFE

Short Stories and Poems

Evelyn Fishler Goldstein

iUniverse, Inc.

New York Lincoln Shanghai

A CLOSE BRUSH WITH LIFE

Short Stories and Poems

Copyright © 2008 by Evelyn Fishler Goldstein

iUniverse books may be ordered through booksellers or by contacting:

iUniverse
2021 Pine Lake Road, Suite 100
Lincoln, NE 68512
www.iuniverse.com
1-800-Authors (1-800-288-4677)

Because of the dynamic nature of the Internet, any Web addresses or links contained in this book may have changed since publication and may no longer be valid.

This is a work of fiction. All of the characters, names, incidents, organizations, and dialogue in these poems and short stories are either the products of the author's imagination or are used fictitiously.

ISBN: 978-0-595-48051-7 (pbk)
ISBN: 978-0-595-60149-3 (ebk)

Printed in the United States of America

In loving memory of my husband and life-collaborator, Irving; and to Rebecca, Richard and Judith—our three best collaborations.

CONTENTS

Preface xiii

POEMS 1

Firelight 1

The Country Dandy 2

The Story Of Lizzie 3

The Race 5

Hello, Goodbye 6

Jimmy 7

No Green Thumb 9

The Seed 10

Take Up Make Up 11

Percival 12

The Big War 13

Mortality 14

A Mirror for My Soul 15

Rainy Days 16

Faithless 17

The House I Lived In 19

Child of The City, I and II 20

Honey and Evy 21

The Days In Color 22

To Judith And Pete 1 23

To Judith And Pete 2 24

Die As In Diet...25

Holidays Today...26

Poems To Teach By 27

At The Dance 34

Creative Writers..35

Salute To The WHOA Folks 36

The Eternal Plan 37

Night Of The Yellow Moon..38

A Song for Irv 40

A Spirited Poem...41

Recollection 43

Not Autobiographical 45

Teachers...46

The Day The Towers Fell 47

Aftermath...48

Before Toys R Us 49

Life 50

Natural Law 51

Beings 52

Hurricane Season 53

Toenail Clipping...54

Dying to Get Slim 55

Golden Years...56

Holiday Spiritless 57

Untitled 58

Stamp Act 59

I'm Not Amused By The Muse 60

Time And The Phantom Horse 61

Vacation's Acumin' 63

The House Without Windows 64

Sighting...65

The Youth And The Dragon 67

"And A Happy New Year to All!" 68

For Those I Love 70

A Poem Of Thanks 71

Dessert Is Not Spelled Desert 72

Hay Fever 73

Ariel 74

Growing Up...76

New World 77

Lonely Heart 78

Outside 79

Speaking Diet-Wise..80

The Cold..81

Mementos 82

The Turkey 83

Imagination...84

Once Upon A Poem..85

Childhood..86

Autobiography 87

The Bee..88

Creative Writing...89

Holidays Today...90

Cloud Pictures..91

The Snows of Yesteryear..92

The Inky-Dink..93

Springtime..94

Unrequited Love 95

Alone 96

Who Is There? 97

Obedience 98

The Toy 99

Jump Frog 100

My Cat 101

Tom And the Genie 102

Not A Lender Nor A Borrower Be 103

Ballerina 104

The Princess And The Witch 105

In The Fall 107

On Stage 108

Once I Knew Love 109

In the Dark 110

Friendship's Loss 112

Storms 113

I Woke In The Morning 114

STORIES 115

The Marry Widow 115

The Sky Is Falling 120

The Worth Of A Man 124

Will Grandma Come Home Again? 129

In Limbo 133

Voices Of Children 141

Mirror, Mirror, On the Wall 147

Abracadabra 151

Abuser 155

Beth's Story 159

Computers—A World I Never Made 162

Found—A Daughter 164

Friendship's Signposts 168

Haven't We Met Before? 171

Kiss Of Depth 174

Let's Talk Turkey 176

Loaf Me Or Knead Me 179

A Christmas Dog Tale 181

Candles In The Snow 183

Cash And Carry 186

Daddy, Why Did You Have To Die? 188

Mouse House 191

On The Platform 192

Parents' Growing-Up Pains 193

Senses Taking 195

Shadow Lover 197

Smother Love 202

Speak Easy In Brooklyn 207

The Devil With Protocol 209

The Girl Inside 211

The Hand Of Love 213

The Mistletoe 217

The Sacrifice 220

Women, Women, Everywhere 225

Nibble, Nibble 230

My Parents Were My Rivals 231

March Of The Toys 235

God Of The Mist 238

The Bird And The Three Wise Men 248

Backyard Alley Cat Queen 250

Preface

There is magic inside us—but we are not always aware of it. This magic is the experience that we have by developing our capabilities. We perform varied functions in many areas of life. We are different things to different people. We accumulate so many abilities that they become automatic and we do not even recognize them as skills. As we utilize our abilities, we enter the magical realm of creativity. Daily life is experienced as a precious gift. At the moment when the magic happens, our work "connects" with others—and creativity transcends our selves, and becomes timeless.

FIRELIGHT

Firelight casts such shadows on the wall,
As makes me think that phantoms came to call.
A horse is rearing up, then crashes down,
And roofs of houses show there is a town.

People dance, or walk about;
The silence whispers, soundless shout—
Soon flames will eat the logs away,
Firelight not long to stay.

And when the room turns cooler soon,
I know that I must leave the room,
And go upstairs, where ceiling light,
Will shine my way all through the night.

Goodbye dear shadows on the wall,
Imagination gave you form,
But now the fire is dying out,
And sleep's erased what you're about.

THE COUNTRY DANDY

Willie was a scoundrel and a gambling man to boot;
And he was a dandy, with shiny boots and stylish suit.
Dark, wavy hair and flashy teeth,
Ladies thought he simply can't be beat,
And invited him inside for some treat.

Willie peddled pushcart wares,
From house dresses to teddy bears;
And was handy with repairs—
Whether buckets or a broken slat in stairs.

What a catch he might have been,
Until a husband caught him sin,
With his wife who thought her hubby out of town.
He found both of them in bed,
And shot poor Willie in the head,
And no jury in the town convicted him.

THE STORY OF LIZZIE

They called her Lizzie the Dizzy.
She wore her brown hair short and frizzy.
She giggled when she spoke,
As though there was a joke,
Though often there was nothing there to laugh at.

In school she wasn't bright;
Her answers rarely right,
And the boys considered her to be a fright.
"Get outa sight! Good night!"

She graduated from high school,
And continued on to college,
Where she showed a sudden aptitude for knowledge.

Her grades were all A's,
And it wasn't just a phase;
For she made the Dean's list,
And she earned much praise.

This success caused her to glow,
And attracted her a beau,
Who declared he loved her so,
That he asked her if she would give
Her hand in marriage.
And a year after they were wed,
She was pushing twin boys in a double carriage.

So you see, a homely child,
Can change as years go by,

Giving hope that life will end with joy
And laughter;

And love, as tales do tell,
Will come round as you know well;
With the lovers living long and happily ever after.

THE RACE

Where are the victors of the race?
They've run and have come face to face;
They trained for weeks to win the game.
Their lungs exploded with their pain.
Many did not come to the fore;
Many fell by the way, their legs too sore.
Those who broke through the rope as first,
Drank much water to quench their thirst.
The winners were blessed; the losers cursed.
In the next contest they will die to be first.
Train through the years and strain to excel,
For that prize of money.
Men will train and strain,
They will burst their hearts,
To win the game.

HELLO, GOODBYE

If I spend the night
Will you be gone?
When I reach out,
For your hand at dawn,
Will you say, I made
No promise to you.

Is it hale, farewell,
No joy, no rue?
A casual kiss—
Then, all is through.

If I spend the night
Will you steal my heart?
Saying, Nothing is
Serious from the start.
No thank-you notes
No fare-thee-well.

Yet, I am bonded
By your spell.
Off you go to your job,
Your wife—
Supposing that I've got my life,
And certain that, as you had planned
It was just to be a one-night stand.

JIMMY

Jimmy laughed and Jimmy giggled.
When he did, his tummy wiggled.
All the kids made fun of him.
Jimmy laughed along with them.
Never showing how much it stung,
To be ridiculed when young.

When Jim grew up into his teens,
Changes came into his genes.
He grew tall and he grew slim,
Surprising all who remembered him.
Females called him on the phone,
Hardly leaving him alone.

He was smart and he was kind,
But he never left behind,
Memories of that lonely boy,
That mockery sought to destroy.
Though his hurt stayed deep inside,
Behind a smiling face he'd hide
The pain that never went away.

Until one sunny, peaceful day,
Jimmy walked to the center of town,
Shooting everybody down.
The last bullet went into his head,
He died without a word being said.
His friends and neighbors said of him,
"No one was as kind and caring as Jim."

And no one ever could explain
Why—without reason—Jim went insane.

NO GREEN THUMB

All 'round my house
Rose bushes grow,
In every color,
They make a show.

And here and there,
An azalea bush,
And a hyacinth
Or a coleus blooms
And I put them in pots,
Inside my rooms.

Unhappily, though one assumes,
I'm capable of making them thrive,
Under my care, they just don't survive.
I can only keep such flowers alive,
Which are made of silk or papier-mâché,
And do not change if I'm home or away.

THE SEED

The little plot of earth she'd tended,
Lost order and its charm seemed ended.
But, to her pleasure, those who passed,
Exclaimed, "How pretty!" and some gasped—
"How did you make a garden spot,
In such an over-weedy plot?"

And she confessed,
"That pretty weed which you do see,
Was never planted by me.
It chose to visit for a while,
To bring to folks a little smile.
Who'd ever think a weed could be,
This pretty flower it came to be?"

But, to her absolute surprise,
Folks seemed to think her enterprise,
Was one she'd planned and dug with spade,
And so a bed of flowers made,

But the wind blew down the random seed,
And her bouquet was—only weed.

TAKE UP MAKE UP

I wake up every morning
And wonder if I'm here.
It's not until my mirror shows
My image very clear.
I see my arms and legs all right;
The morning face gives me a fright.

I need the make-up, base and lotions,
Which I call my magic potions,
Changing from the witch I'm seeing,
To a normal human being.

So, don't begrudge cosmetic spending
To help attain my happy ending.
I prefer I not be seen,
In July, like Halloween.

PERCIVAL

Percy is a little white dog
Of royal pedigree.
He's bonded to his mistress,
With little care for me.
His buddy is a big black chow,
More haughty and more mellow.
Who'd rather be with humans,
Than another doggie fellow.

So, when the mistress leaves the house,
Perce sits at the door like
A patient mouse.
His happiest times are when
Mistress and master,
Return from an errand
A great deal faster.

Percy's life then seems
Complete, as he
Parks himself lovingly down
At their feet,
And the only thing happier
Is getting a treat;
Or when dinner is served and
He gets something to eat.

THE BIG WAR

In the best of time,
There was fragile peace.
And the people prayed,
It would never cease.
But small wars there were,
And some revolutions.
To slow the growth of evolutions.

Despite this, progress forged ahead.
People had jobs and were well fed.
They married and planned their future years,
With happy times and times of tears.

But when the Big War finally came,
Nothing was ever again the same.
Lives were changed;
Futures rearranged.
Histories tell how this came to be,
And why there's no you—
No one but me.

MORTALITY

A child is running down the street.
Jealously, I watch his feet
Pumping without effort or strain
Unaware of age or pain.

"When I was young," I wanted to say,
"I, too, ran swiftly through each day.
What a spendthrift I have been,
Empty days are such a sin!"

Childhood's gone and youth is wasted,
Leaving luxuries untasted.
How did all those years get spent?
Working hard to pay the rent?

Raising children the best we can,
Childhood goes and then the man.
Here you stand where a child has run,
Thinking how soon your life is done.

Will there ever be another again?
Such beliefs give hope to men.
The genes that created you unique,
Won't ever be found, wherever you seek.

So—do your living at the highest plane.
What it is you are, won't be ever again!

A MIRROR FOR MY SOUL

I wish that one day I could see
The hidden side that's really me.
The side that's pretty, witty, cute.
And looks just right in a bathing suit.
Boo-hoo my mirror will not lie,
Whatever side I turn and try.

One day I'll pass a magic shop,
And there I'll definitely stop
To buy a mirror made for me,
To show how I would wish to be.

RAINY DAYS

Rainy days are good for this—
For indoor chores I often miss;
Cleaning house, baking pies,
Walking the rooms to thin my thighs.

These are plans toward which I look.
Instead, I sit down with a book,
And when the hours have passed away,
Dark comes on with the end of day.

I sigh because I've squandered time—
Berate myself like it's a crime.
But when the years have quickly passed,
I've come to realize at last,

Those were my golden hours and days,
When I broadened my mind in wonderful ways.
Today, with the burden of my daily job,
Of book reading time, I know I feel robbed.

These days there's a different path for me,
And it is known as ... watching TV.

FAITHLESS

The night is dark,
But I cannot sleep;
My love is far away.

Where have you gone,
My long lost darling?
Why have you gone astray?

You left our bed,
In the early morn,
Leaving me lonely and forlorn.

I watched at the window,
And stood at the door,
But you never came back,
As you came back before.

If something had happened
To you on the road,
I would have this dire feeling,
Of loss, of forebode.

But I know well, my dear,
Of your roving eye;
And the smile of a lady,
Will make you stop by.

And you'll dally the night long,
Forgetting that I,
Will stand at the window,
And watch at the door,

'Till your returning
To my arms once more.

THE HOUSE I LIVED IN

I lived in a house for fifty years,
A house of joy, a house of tears;
A house of childhood growing up,
Where love's first sorrow filled my cup.

Most carefree time I'll ever know,
Where idealism was the way to go.
I believed in good; at evil I raged,
But not quite full was every page.

I learned to take things moderately,
Realizing vast joys can't truly be.
But sadness comes with enormity.
I've no belief in an after-time,

Since those I've lost never gave a sign.
I only think: Do the best you can;
Live like a child;
Grow up like a man.

CHILD OF THE CITY, I AND II

I.

I am a child of the city.
When I was very young,
I saw trees—only in picture books.

Now I am grown.
Where I live,
There are trees—climbing out of concrete.

I wonder
How many other children
In the world grow old without seeing a tree?

II.

I would like to give you a birthday gift,
Trees and flowers and breaking waves.
I would like your soul and spirits to lift,
Seeing hills of green and lime-wet hidden caves.

If you have seen them all—and paid no mind,
Living your life, all busy and filled,
No one can fault you or call you blind,
For living your life as you have willed.

Not everybody needs nature's sights,
To inspire them to rise above their birth,
Some fortunate people can reach great heights,
Just by the way they live on the Earth.

HONEY AND EVY

She was my best friend.
Her name was Honey.
Blond hair. Blue eyes.
She was considered bonny.
And being pretty, she liked the boys.
She married early to a gambling man,
Who squandered her earnings as fast as he can.

I began to write—
Poems and stories were my delight.
Once upon a time I wrote
Fairy tales I'd often quote.
Enchanted tales I loved to read,
And hoped in writing I'd succeed.

I even wrote books, which didn't do well;
And occasionally a work I managed to sell.
So here today are works I treasure.
Writing because it gives me pleasure.
No one will know me in the years ahead,
But I'll write for enjoyment,
Until I am dead.

While pretty Honey, I'm sorry to say,
Lost her good looks and soon passed away.
She had little of interest and spent her days,
Viewing TV from morning to night.
And I was the one who was left to weep,
When they phoned to say Honey died in her sleep.

THE DAYS IN COLOR

The lilacs and the purples,
And the pinks of sunset's glow,
Cast rosy light on buildings,
And on sidewalks down below.

The faces of the people,
Reflected in twilight grow,
Shadowed as the dusk,
Darkens to night below.

The end of day,
Has lost its way,
And lost the color gray.

Without the street lamps,
Dusk is dark,
And folks could lose their way.

Work's done,
And night's for going home—
To sleep,
To love,
To close your eyes,
And hope for happy dreams at night,
And lovely glows with dawn's sunrise.

TO JUDITH AND PETE 1

This is the time I must say, "Thank you!"
You are lovingly thoughtful,
In all that you do.
Since I've come to visit you in icy-cold Mass,
You have a heater in the car, to warm up my ass.
Now that really treats a person first-class.
And so I must tell you before this is through,
How very dearly I really love you!
And if you ask—if you're too shy to guess,
The answer is yes, yes, yes, yes, yes....

To Judith And Pete 2

The time has come to say good-bye,
I wipe a teardrop from my eye.
I've had a great time as guest in your home,
If you are out working, I'm still not alone.
Nimbus the cat sits on my bed,
Waiting for me to scratch her head.
And Percy watches at the door,
Eager to greet your return once more.

I kind of hang out ... the dogs not sure what for.
But one more human they seem to endure.
Though they sometimes shy off, as though they're not sure.
I wonder if when I return to Orlando,
The dogs will miss me, or maybe not know,

If the human who petted their heads
Was ever really a visitor there?
Will they think about me? Or forget?
Or will they simply not give a care?

DIE AS IN DIET

I love cake and candy,
And all kinds of pies.
But my doctor reminds me,
Such foods are not wise.
They will make me expand,
To a much greater size.

I must use self-control,
And full well realize,
I can devour all desserts,
But,
Only with my eyes.

HOLIDAYS TODAY

The children were with us
When we were all young;
Joining in songs,
We had always sung.

They carried the years,
Like melting snow,
Out of our house,
When they chose to go.

Our mirrors are frozen,
In splinters of scenes,
Stirred up by photos,
And unbidden dreams.

The table is empty,
Snuff candlelight;
Festivities ended;
Prepare for the night....

POEMS TO TEACH BY

Abou Ben Adhem by Leigh Hunt

Abou ben Adhem, may his pay increase,
Awoke one night from a deep dream of peace,
And quickly for pen and paper ran,
He'd forgotten to write his weekly lesson plan.

I Saw A Ship Asailing by Robert Louis Stevenson

I saw a ship a-sailing,
A-sailing on the sea,
But taxes and deductions,
Make it sail off—without me.

North Wind

The north wind doth blow,
And we shall have snow,
And what will poor teacher do then, poor thing?
She'll sit out the storm,
And try to keep warm,
For they used all the coal up last spring, last spring.

The Village Blacksmith by Longfellow

Under a spreading chestnut tree,
Arbor Day program is planned.
The band strikes up a lively tune,
There's a spade in the Principal's hand.
The speeches are ready,
And everything's set,

When the heavens suddenly open,
And everyone gets wet.

To Market, To Market—by Mother Goose

To market, to market
To buy mutual shares,
Cost of living is rising,
So pensioner prepares.

Sing A Song Of Sixpence—by Mother Goose

Sing a song of six cents
For cookies class must pay.
What is teacher supposed to do?
Each child brought a dime today!

Fairy Song by John Keats

Shed no tear! O, shed no tear!
More flowers will bloom another year,
Didn't you know when you left plants there,
None would survive the holiday care?

Excelsior by William Wordsworth

The window shades were closing fast
As through our halls a monitor passed,
A youth who bore a packaged gift,
Supposed to give the teacher a lift,
But what was hidden deep within,
Made the wrapping just a sin!
A tiny vase, inside a crate,

It hardly was worth all that weight
To fill a classroom—wall to door
With all that darn
EXCELSIOR!

The Rainbow by William Wordsworth

My heart leaps up,
When I behold,
That snow has come our way,
If it keeps up throughout the night,
There won't be school next day.

All's Right With The World by Robert Browning

The year's at the Spring,
And day's at the morn;
Iowa Test time,
Makes students forlorn.

My Shadow by Robert L. Stevenson

I have a little shadow,
That goes in and out with me,
Asking at each classroom door,
"Did you find my teacher's key?"

A Psalm Of Life by Longfellow

Lives of great men, all remind us,
We can make our lives sublime.

Just return the gym key promptly,
And get class out of gym on time.

Trees by Joyce Kilmer

I think that I shall never see, a window shade that works for me:
A shade that darkens when I say,
"We're viewing movies, class, today."
A cord that won't—in pulling—tear,
And let in sunshine everywhere;
A shade that does not—in the gloom,
Give way and light the whole classroom.

Projectors are run by fools like me,
But only the shade can make us see.

Oh Where, Oh Where....

Oh where, oh where, has the TV gone?
Oh where, oh where, can it be?
Our science program was scheduled for ten,
But we didn't find it till three!

Gradatim by Josiah Gilbert Holland

Heaven is not reached at a single bound,
Except when class records you lost, are found.

Evangeline by Longfellow

This is the forest primeval,
The murmuring teacher drinks hemlock,

Pile-up of books leaves her nearly deranged,
It's that time in June when books are exchanged

Woodman, Spare That Tree

Woodman, spare that desk!
Carve not your name on it!
In class you doodle there,
That is—when I got you to sit!

Song by John Donne

Go and catch a falling star;
Our class play lead,
Stepped from the stage too far.

The Night Before Christmas by C. Moore

"Twas the night before conference,
And all through the school
Most teachers were standing with hammer on stool,
Best papers were hung on the bulletins with care,
And the hopes that most parents,
Would fail to be there.

Tiger, Tiger! by William Blake

Tiger, tiger, burning bright
Hot with anger and a sight
Because you got into a fight,
And a riot did incite.

Do you think, Oh Mighty Mite,
At age of six that that is right?

Upon Looking Into Chapman's Homer by John Keats

Then felt I like some watcher of the skies,
Because a child let the swinging door,
Bring stars unto my eyes.

Children's Hour by Longfellow

Between the dark and the daylight,
When the night is beginning to lower,
Comes the ordeal, which all teacher's know
As Parent Conference Hour.

When I Was One And Twenty by A.E. Houseman

When I was one and twenty,
I heard a wise man say,
"Give paper, pencils, thumb tacks
But never a manual away!"

With Rue My Heart Is Laden by A.E. Houseman

With rue my heart is laden,
My checkbook is a sight,
I got my pay—less pension—
So this month we eat light.

From Macbeth by Shakespeare

Out! Out, damn spot!
You know the teacher's roll book,
Can't have a single blot!

Hi, Diddle Diddle by Mother Goose

Hi, diddle diddle, the boy and the fiddle,
Music teacher's beginning to foam,
But the whole class laughed to see such sport,
Concert night he left instrument home!

Thirty Days Hath September

Thirty days hath September,
April, June and November,
February we all love best,
All other months we do detest,
The other months are all accursed,
Because paycheck is given on the FIRST!

AT THE DANCE

Did you think that when I went away
It was something that I chose?
Why would I ever leave you?
Can you guess? Can you suppose?

We'd go out to a dance
And you would flirt with other girls—
The dark-haired or the red heads;
Straight-haired, or ones with curls.

I'd sit at a seat against the wall,
And off you'd go like I'm not there at all.
And the girls would all give you the eye,
As you smiled at them and passed me by.

But if I accepted another man's dance,
You'd cut in quickly, not to give him a chance.
You need to know that I am through
Waiting for a dance with you.

The next man who says he'll take me home
Will find me willing to leave you alone.
So don't expect me to sit and wait,
And hope that you will phone.

I'm leaving 'cause I'm better off
To live my life alone.

CREATIVE WRITERS

I read once,
That science has found,
The end of our Universe.

If that is so,
Then we are there, my friends,
Fashioning young worlds,
Out of our mind thoughts.

Creating star matter,
Novas and nebulae,
Showerworks of meteors,
Fire molten earths;

Bursting the vacuums
Of dark stars and quarks,
Scattering out galaxies …
Shrinking the darks.

SALUTE TO THE WHOA FOLKS

(Williamsburg Homeowners Association, Orlando, FL)

Williamsburg began to rise,
 Where the wild grass had free space;
 Where the armadillos dug,
 And the geckos marked their place.
 Where the sun-warmed rocks could offer
 Resting places for the snakes,
 And wild turkey strolled unchallenged,
 And the bovines dropped dung-cakes.

Now the Seniors live and flourish,
 Where the wildlife once were nourished.

Live a happy Golden Age,
 You have earned the Center Stage.

THE ETERNAL PLAN

I plan to live forever,
I told my family and friends.
I just must figure out,
How this can come about.

It's hard to live a full life,
Yet keep from getting old.
Even if I cream my face
The wrinkles find a newer place.

Dye may keep my hair from gray,
And diet keep the flab away
Moisturizing skin galore,
Tightens up my every pore.
But when all's done, I'm as before.
And nothing stops the final score.

I'll never have my youth again.
That went away, I don't know when.
But if I keep my health intact,
That's the best I can ask,
As a matter of fact.

NIGHT OF THE YELLOW MOON

On the night of the yellow moon,
Cathy fell in love.
Stars shone like fireflies
In the dark sky above.

She was seventeen and Jim was twenty-four;
But Cathy knew this man she would worship and adore.
She knew that he was married
And lately fathered a child.
None of that mattered,
His smile drove poor Cathy wild.

He had curly black hair,
His eyes were deep blue.
His gaze always seemed especially for you.
He could have had any girl in the town.
But he was faithful to Mary and turned all others down.

"Oh, Jim, I do love you!" poor Cathy cried.
"Another will come and you'll push me aside."
She never believed this could ever come to be,
'Till the dance at the social when Sam said:
"Dance with me."

Light as a feather, in his arms she did whirl;
He made her feel like the most beautiful girl.
Jim totally went out of her thoughts and her head,
And soon to her Sam happily was wed.

Years later to her daughter, Cathy wisely said:
"Don't fall for good looks when you're ready to wed.

Search for the man who is kind and is true;
And then happiness in life will always be there for you."

A Song for Irv

No, I'm not ready for the Ball,
I know my escort's coming soon,
But I'm not ready, not at all.

I wish you'd clear the room
Of all my friends and family,
Dressed in their best to escort me.
But—I'm not ready for the Ball,
And just refuse to go at all!

Don't send me cards, or bring bouquets.
Save those for some later days.
The band's struck up the funeral tune,
All I can say is—"It is too soon!"

A Spirited Poem

Tis the time of the spirits
And costumes and paints,
And devilish tricks

On this night called All Saints.
The kids ask their parents,
For make-up and sheets,
And baskets for bringing home
Money and treats.

They sail through the night,
Little ghosts, little witches,
And ring neighbors' doorbells,
And make the same pitches.

Some leave off their masks
Not to scare folks they know.
Trick or treating
Is all a part of the show.

By supper when baggies
Are dumped of their loot,
Of money and candies
And even some fruit,

Many a ghost and many a witch,
Wish they'd had less luck
In making their pitch.
Halloween's fun when you're
Out with a friend,

But when tummy aches come,
It's a devilish end.

RECOLLECTION

There are not many things that I recall;
A childhood—loved and cared for—but uncertain;
Not sure, in my mind that I was capable,
That I could speak and gain attention.

When I was young—a childlike child,
If I spoke up, the folks would laugh.
How could I know they pleasured in me?
I only thought they laughed at me.

So—adults were a fearsome thing.
And I was shy and ready to hide,
Sure that they made mockery of all I'd say.

Now I am old and look back down the years
Of time—gone faster than the speed of sound.
I wish I'd known that love was not just hugs and kisses.
But laughter and delight of what a child did say.

Let me speed back through my lifetime—
Tell that child I used to be:
"Don't dismay at youth's confusion.
You'll grow older, all too soon.

'Till one day the pace you've traveled,
Will accelerate to age—
Leaving you to stand and wonder,
How life passed while you were living,
Never knowing it passed by.

Goodbye, child at the telescope's end,
Far and small and dwindling out,

Life has left you at its stage front,
Living out a special part.

When the curtain starts its closing,
Will you know you've left a trail—
Like a comet swiftly passing,
From the birthing to the veil?"

NOT AUTOBIOGRAPHICAL

Hey, old lady with the cane,
Walking slowly up the lane,
Taking frequent stops to rest,
Sometimes holding hands to chest.

Dreaming of the younger days,
Bow in hair was then the rage,
Bobby socks, blouses and skirts
College dances—loves and hurts;

Mama with her stove and pot,
Papa reading books a lot;
Siblings telling of their days;
Company—it seemed—always.

Now the picture's not the same;
Lonely days and nights of pain.
Poor old lady, pity thee.
Hey, old lady—you are ME!

TEACHERS

Hundreds of children I have taught,
Good little kids and those that fought.
Age has brought my life up short,
Have those years all gone for naught?

I can only hope that I
Made a difference 'ere I die.
Otherwise, I'll wonder why,
I was chosen to pass by.

THE DAY THE TOWERS FELL

The air above the storm is calm,
But man-made storms have little charm.
A man-made holocaust out of the sky,
Changed our world in the blink of an eye.

Hijacked planes hit our proudest towers,
Sending down bricks and debris like showers;
Turning our giants of steel and glass
To powders that littered and blackened our grass.

This is an enemy we never can sate—
This bitter evil that we know as HATE!

AFTERMATH

We don't sleep as we used to sleep.
We wake in the night and begin to weep.
Our world was changed by an enemy's stealth,
Ordered by a terrorist of incredible wealth—

Born to a religion that teaches love,
He made sacrifice of the white peace dove.
He crashed our towers and ashed our city,
This man without mercy, or justice, or pity.

He taught us a lesson we'll never forget—
Love your neighbors, but keep alarms set!

BEFORE TOYS R US

There was magical joy
In a can-top toy
In the long ago days
Of my youth.
Momma would wash the can off clean,
And give the top to me.
No happier child could ever be seen,
As out to the street I'd go
Bend the lid in half,
Holding it fast with my toe,
Stamp with my heel
For a flattened feel,
And when it was triangle flat,
I'd pitch it on a pavement block,
Keeping it off any crack!
Hop to kick to the very next square,
Careful, so pals don't shout, "Not fair!"

Now that I'm grown and buying kid toys,
I always tell my own little boys:
Nothing brings a child such joy,
As making his very own can-top toy.
The toy that brought such joy to me
And which, at that time, we called:
"Potsy!"

LIFE

Birthdays come and birthdays go,
Like an avalanche of snow,
And you cannot holler Whoa!
To slow down the overflow!

Youth, you thought would never end—
Nor family love, nor your best friend;
Schoolday chums and work-place ties,
Reel like movies, past your eyes.

You meet your mate,
You set the date,
And live your life as planned by fate.

You think you've done it all your way,
With no-one else to say you nay.
But, in the end, who is to know
The Planner who produced your show.

NATURAL LAW

If this universe was created
    By a BIG BANG out in space,
And all matter's built and torn down,
    Is it a wonder the human race,
Dies in wartime, lives in peace?
    And our history shows this process
Just continues without cease.

BEINGS

This is a different time and place;
This is a different kind of race,
    Wars and fighting don't take place.

Where's this nation?
    Where's this place?
Nowhere near the human race.

Ours is a Universe born in turbulence;
    Build and tear down is the law,
If creation needs destruction,
    Isn't our destiny then—peace and war?

HURRICANE SEASON

Wait! No, not another one
Is spawning in the ocean—
Filling folks with fear and panicky emotion.
All the news we hear is how
Another hurricane is forming,
And whether it will reach the land,
By night or early morning.

There's exodus from mobile homes,
And pet needs to be planned for.
There's need to fasten windows closed,
And border up the door.
Can't take the cherished heirloom quilt,
And other things of treasure.
All thoughts are for the safety needs,
And that's the foremost measure.
Just pray the roof does not fly off,
And leave all inundated.

Suspense is high while hurricanes,
Are fearfully awaited.
And finally, when storm has passed,
And you are homeward due,
The news arrives that yet another storm
Has spawned and coming through.

TOENAIL CLIPPING

Sitting in the doctor's chair,
Hoping he'll soon be aware,
That I'm really truly there.
Door is open. He flits by—
Sometimes he will say, "Oh, Hi!"
Doesn't stop 'cause off he goes,
To tend to someone else's toes.
Why can't I wait in the waiting room,
Where my folks expect me pretty soon?
Wouldn't they be shocked to know,
Clippers haven't touched my toe!

DYING TO GET SLIM

He walked the treadmill faithfully,
To try to lose some weight.
He counted calories each meal,
Was careful what he ate.
He stayed a tall and slender man,
And then what was his fate?

He met a pretty gourmet cook,
They fell in love with just one look;
Their marriage was a happy thing.
She treated him just like a king.
And he got rounder with each meal,
And lost his slender sex appeal.

Still happily, he ate away,
And to his friends he'd simply say:
"It seems to be a mortal fate,
As we grow old we put on weight."
And when he died the tombstone state
Was—"Now his problem's not with weight."

GOLDEN YEARS

I've walked along this street before—
    A neighbor is behind each door.
I say "Hello" when someone's out
    Or—from a window hear a shout;
"How you doing? You okay?"
"Doing fine" is what I say.

If we stop and talk a while,
    Truth comes out—I lose my smile.
"Pains in joints. Need surgery."
"Getting treatments—hip and knee."
"Have a stiffness in my neck!"
"Boy! I feel like such a wreck!"
    Oh, I really sympathize
With those pains from neck to thighs.

When we moved here ten years back,
    And settled in our cul-de-sac,
    We conversed of kin or cat,
    And rarely spoke of ills like that.

Getting old should come with health.
    'Twouldn't hurt—if also wealth!
Doctors, hurry with those genes,
    That can make us feel like teens.
We don't have much time to wait.
    Speed's what we'd appreciate.

HOLIDAY SPIRITLESS

This is the season of holiday cheer;
    Why does it make me unhappily drear?
Family's far off. I live by myself.
    I'd be glad of the company of even an elf.

I shouldn't complain;
    My friends are so dear,
It's just no fun alone,
    Any season of the year.

UNTITLED

Dying will come on one day,
Preferably not right away;
We prefer it far away.
Next millennium's okay.

STAMP ACT

The price of first class mail goes higher;
The stamps are issued, but the buyer
Must commit to memory
The requested postal fee.
'Cause the government doesn't tell you,
The value of the stamps they sell you.

We can't protest, or know who to blame,
When stamps are issued without name.
Petitions we would gladly aim,
If we could know the culprit's name.

So, we buy the stamps and pay the price,
And grumble that it just ain't nice
That we must pay and take a licking,
Hoping that the stamps are sticking.

If the stamps must rise in price,
Candy flavor would be nice.

I'm Not Amused By The Muse

Alas, I did not write a thing,
And do not have a poem to bring.
I thought up rhymes I felt were cool,
While I walked to the swimming pool.

Why is it that the Muse bears fruit,
When I am in my bathing suit?
And there isn't a pencil or a pad in sight,
'Till I'm toweled dry—but forgot what to write!

TIME AND THE PHANTOM HORSE

Across the street of Tim's bedroom view,
Was a desolate tenement, none remembered as new.
And time saw in the window, in the cracks of the glass,
A shadow outline of a horse, running fast.
Its ears were pricked back and its mouth white with foam;
No rider astride him to urge him to home.

"Come here and I'll ride you," Tim called to the steed,
Who whinnied as though he sure meant to accede.
But Tim knew no matter how deeply he'd care,
There was no way he ever could leave his wheelchair.

His mom was concerned and the doctor was too,
That Tim's heard was too weak to let him pull through.
But Tim made a wish, which no one could give,
To ride the tenement horse as long as he had to live.

In his dreams he would, ride with his hands in the mane,
No saddle beneath him, not even a rein.
Bareback, he would travel, with incredible speed,
No traffic on highways, just he and his steed.
They'd dash past each home and each school and each store,
With people astounded as never before.
Folks would cheer and they'd wave Timmy on—
So fast was his riding that soon he was gone.

The townsfolk were puzzled by what they had seen,
And only conjectured on what it could mean.
While back in his room, dark coming at last,
Tim felt strength return and pain leaving fast.

His movements were easier. Gone shortness of breath.
And he leapt to the back of the steed known as Death.

VACATION'S ACUMIN'

I've waiting all year for vacation time.
I would spend it in traveling, but haven't a dime.
As I worked, I just spent the amount that I earned.
A bitter lesson I have learned.

Now I stay home and do ordinary things—
Writing letters, or taking the phone when it rings.
Doing laundry each week; walking the dog twice a day,
When I could have been traveling to lands far away.

Next year I will certainly plan in advance,
And not leave vacation to frivolous chance.
Though I put every penny I have in a jar,
Or into my bank, which is not very far—
I will save. I will stint—
Though it won't be a mint—

It will just be enough to allow me to go,
Wherever the four winds may happen to blow;
And my traveling money will surely allow,
Expenses to be covered so I can go now.

Farewell to sameness and to routine.
I'm off to places I never have seen.
I'm off to follow a lifetime dream.

And when I am home and working again,
I'll save my money so next year when
I go on vacation that I can afford,
Like a squirrel, with nuts for his next winter hoard,
My savings, I too, will have nutfully stored.

THE HOUSE WITHOUT WINDOWS

Across the street the house has been
Empty forever, or so it would seem.
Shutters are missing, or dangling down,
On this most desolated house in our town.

The boys throw their stones to see who is best
At breaking more panes than all of the rest.
Policemen night-chase those young vandals away,
But when they are gone, the boys come back to play.

Then one day a limo drove down the street,
And out stepped a lady as pale as a sheet.
She wept as she saw the demolished old house,
From which there did scurry a resident mouse.

"Long years ago this house was brand new.
I lived with my folks here till age twenty-two.
Then, one day, when driving, they were killed in their car,
And I went to my grandma who lived very far.

But once in a while I come back once more,
To find the house crumpling worse than before."
And weeping as ever she drove off in her car,
To the new life she lived now, however so far.

But the boys stopped ball-tossing at each windowpane,
'Till construction men tore every brick down again.
One day on the lot there was building begun,
And a high-rise apartment stopped all the boys' fun.

And some who now live there do often exclaim,
"In the shadows of twilight shimmers a house with no pane."

SIGHTING

The flying object skimmed spiraling down from the sky;
No noise of motor to tell us why.
We watched how it wobbled to a landing site;
Much like the reeling down of a kite.
Dad rushed to get his camera out.
Our dog Kip frantically whirled about
Barking and cowering and not sure what to do.
A flying saucer was nothing he or I knew.

Where were the reporters?
The camera men? The press?
Were my family and I
The only ones who knew
A strange flying object had come into view?

Mother picked up the telephone
Dialing 9-1-1, saying, "We're not alone!"
An object has landed from out-of-space,
And what's inside we're afraid to face.

Is it a human, a robot or what?
When it comes from the vessel will it frightening be?
Or will it look human—like you and like me?

Oh my, there's an opening, there, from the side.
A long-legged figure walks out with stiff stride.
And when he confronts me his hands go up in greeting.
And right then I knew we were like two friends meeting.
I held out my hand and was grasped in firm clasp.
"To a new future of friendship and one that will last!"

That was ten years ago that the aliens came.
Human life is no longer the same.
They've settled among us—
Humans and They.
We've become compatible in every way.

The human race has more mighty grown,
With the addition of strength from the alien clone.
Now we are breeding a much better race,
Like Greek gods in body and beauty of face.

The meeting of humans and outer space folk
Are the seeds of new myths
About which legends spoke.

THE YOUTH AND THE DRAGON

"The way is steep," the old hag said,
"The paths are lined with bones of the dead.
Go back and find an easier life,
The way you chose is bloodied with strife."

But youth is filled with confidence,
Certain no task is too immense.
Besides, the rewards are great with glory,
And legends will sing a hero's story.

When one is only seventeen,
And is offered a crown and a beauteous queen,
To slay a dragon seems worth the chance,
To ask the Devil for his hand in a dance.

And so the lad, as others had done,
Sought his foe, shouting, "I am the one
Who will slay you before this evening is done."

And out came the dragon, breathing hot fire,
And extinguished the young laddie's courage and desire.
Then went to the lake, his great self to admire.

The slaying of mortals sometimes can tire
Even great dragons born to breathe fire.

"AND A HAPPY NEW YEAR TO ALL!"

The holidays are coming,
And presents come to me.
I check my list and nearly faint,
When this is what I see:
I sent a gift to Aunt Marie,
Who never sent a gift to me.
Forgot to contact Cousin Bea,
Who sent a nineteen-inch TV.

My wealthy cousins from the West,
Who always claimed they loved me best,
Mailed out a check they'd hoped I'd use,
For anything I'd care to choose.
Some friends gave me expensive booze,

And happily, I think,
Felt I'd imbibe—not knowing
That I'm not allowed to drink.
Angora sweaters, chiffon scarves,
And blouses sized too small for me,
Came all wrapped up with bows that tied,
But were too narrow, or too wide.

How sad they spent such time and trouble,
Hunting through so many stores.
I'm sure they wore their soles out, trudgin'
All those polished floors.

And now my four-foot tree is ready to be lit,
And round me are the packages, while on the floor I sit,
Discarding all the ribboning, the gift wrap and the string,
And diligent, I list the names to go with everything.

And finally, when Christmas goes and is no longer here,
I'm tired, but want to wish you all,
A HAPPY, HEALTHY, SAFE NEW YEAR!

FOR THOSE I LOVE

I wish for fame and fortune,
And friends who are close and care,
And health until my dying day,
And love for all to share.

If I could have a magic lamp,
To wish this to come true,
I'd also ask, if possible,
To share this all with you.

A Poem Of Thanks

How clever: the weather,
That knows when to shine,
And rains on the crops,
To make them grow fine.

And blows off the clouds,
So the sun can shine through,
Making pleasant the day,
For our work to pursue.

In rain or in shine,
We learn to survive,
Breathing deep—giving thanks,
And so glad we're alive!

DESSERT IS NOT SPELLED DESERT

Cheesecake is a favorite dish,
And carrot cake is quite delish.
Sponge cake's great with strawberries and cream,
Marble cake is a gourmet chef's dream.
Pudding cakes are a lip-smacking treat;
There's just no dessert that's too rich to eat.

But after your scale has told your weight,
Calorie counting becomes your sad fate.
Taking it off is much harder to achieve,
So simply say no and then sit there and grieve.

Give up your pies, your puddings, your bread.
You may lose the weight, but wish you were dead.

HAY FEVER

My thumb's not green,
I'm sad to say,
Can't make flowers grow,
In any way.
Daren't even smell a picked bouquet,
Or nose will run,
Like hell to pay.
And so my home,
In every room,
Has pots of flowers,
That never bloom.
And trees that only look like real,
And all to help me to conceal,
My need to sneeze,
Despite false trees,
Which happily have eye appeal.

ARIEL

When Rae gave birth to Ariel,
The baby's beauty was like a spell.
Folks said they surely never did see,
A babe of such exquisite beauty.
"She's just an angel," they all exclaimed,
And Ariel she was rightly named.

But the doctor was worried,
When his check-up of things,
Showed the tiny protrusion of possible wings.
What the birth certificate might have revealed,
The doctor thought wisely was better concealed.
With Ariel's mother he held secret discussion,
And agreed revelation was nothing to rush in.

But, as Ariel grew, her winglets did too,
Which made secrecy somewhat of a stew.
The doctor ousted gym from Ariel's locker,
Where dressing with others would cause quite a shocker.
Besides having talent, mom was also quite wise.
She designed all the clothes with the skill to disguise,
That under the garments, whose style was correct,
Lay feathery wings none would ever suspect.

Her classmates were not sure what there was about her,
But were uneasy enough to seriously doubt her.
And so none of the girls called her up on the phone,
Or asked her to join them when they were at home.
Indeed, it did seem that she was quite alone,

Except for the fact that the boys in her class,
Ignored a boy—Timmy—not one, but en masse.

On prom night Tim asked Ariel for a date,
Which turned out to be a good stroke of fate,
For they danced every dance only with each other,
And that roomful of people could see he did love her.
None were surprised when they said they would wed,
And plans for the wedding went quickly ahead.
When questioned of honeymooning, the two simply smiled,
In spite of curiosity that had the town wild.

When they stood at the altar and vowed honor and love,
Guests heard angel music from the heaven above.
And when they threw rice at the bride and groom,
As they flung the bouquet and raced from the room,
Witnesses swore they saw the wings on their backs,
As they flew into night without leaving tracks.

Sure they were joining other winged folk,
They became a town legend of which everyone spoke.
And in the clear nights when folks see a shooting star,
They point and exclaim, "That's where Ariel and Tim are."

GROWING UP

Here I am in high-heeled shoes,
Stepping dainty where I choose.
Pirouetting down the room,
Dancing with my mommie's broom.

I can be whoever I wish,
As I give the skirt a swish.
This is me in big sister's gown,
While she's honeymooning, out of town.

I don't think it's any sin,
Playing that I'm sister's twin.
I know that it's just pretend—
Out the door it all will end.

Mom says one day I'll be grown,
And wishing back this time I own,
So I come here every day,
And—"Grown-Up" is what I play.

Strange that adults envy me.
When I'm grown,
Will I agree?

NEW WORLD

This is the new world I inhabit;
Crane, sandpiper, egret, rabbit.
All stroll casually down my lane.
Turkeys tap at my glass door pane.

Geckos race in swift and small,
Eager to climb my kitchen wall.
Armadillos dig up my grass;
Mounts of fire ants lurk where I pass.

It's enough to make my hair curl,
Considering I am a city-born girl.

LONELY HEART

I wear my heart in my eyes,
But you never realize,
Take my hand and follow me;
There are wonders we should see.

Rainbows in a cloudless sky,
Birds building nests,
How swift they fly.
Why does everyone have some other?
I, alone need to discover,

Someone who is right for me.
Someone who my mate will be.
I await, but where is he?
Romancing someone who is not me.

OUTSIDE

If a friend plans a party,
But does not invite you,
Are you sad? Are you blue?

You may think you're not smart,
As those you know were asked.
Or perhaps one more guest just adds to the hosts' task.

You may think that you're not worthy,
Not competent, or good.
And you feel yourself belittled,
As you most definitely should.

SPEAKING DIET-WISE

All my life I tried to diet.
If you don't think it's tough
    You ought to try it.
Counting calories may sound like fun.
    Maybe, when you've first begun.
But after weeks with little success,
    You feel your life is just a mess.

Then along came carbs—a new device.
    To cause your shape look extra nice.
Two-hundred carbs per day, I'm told.
    Much too much food for my tummy to hold!

My dietician is slim and tall.
    Can't bond with dumpy me, at all.
But blithely, she this diet prescribed.
    Which will make me the fattest skeleton alive.

No bones you'll find, though you poke my skin.
    Carbs isn't a diet to make you thin.
It mainly is to down the sugar in me.
    And has no effect on my plump tummy.

So I follow my diet, while tears fill my cup,
    Knowing sugar may drop, but my scale goes up.

THE COLD

I COUGH; I SNEEZE,
    And in my chest I hear a wheez.
I gargle and I swallow pills,
    Which only slightly help my ills.

This cold, I know will run its course,
    And I'll forget I was even hoarse.
But, while it's with me, you can see,
    I'm in a lot of misery.

If science gets us to Pluto and Mars,
    And telescopes scan the far-off stars,
How long must I age; how long grow old,
    Before they find a cure for the common cold?

MEMENTOS

I cook and I clean
And I dust and I sweep.
All my mementos
I treasure and keep.

I forget as the days go,
Years are passing, too.
And suddenly my collections,
Someone else will go through.

My heirs will need to come here, I expect,
And look over the mishmash of what I collect.
They'll look at each item with far different eyes,
And not give the same fondness to things that I prize.

Why a fuzzy dog with dirty, torn ears,
That I slept with and treasured for all my young years,
Casts magic for me, which for others disappears....
Or else it really just never was there,
Despite polish and dusting and my loving care.

And yet—I just cannot toss out in the bin,
Those treasures invited by me to come in.
I just gather about me those trophies, but then,
Put them out to recycle by indiff'rnt garbage men.

THE TURKEY

The turkey is a useful bird, although his song is rarely heard.
He runs or walks with a kind of wobble,
Often saying, "Gobble, gobble."

Although he's fed to be quite fat,
He's quite content to be just that.
He doesn't know he'll be the winner
Of the centerpiece at Thanksgiving.

So, Mr. Turkey, enjoy your life,
And just ignore the sharpening knife.

IMAGINATION

Mornings as I brush and floss,
Tales and poems, my mind will cross.
Often by the time I'm dressed,
Thoughts on paper I've expressed.

Nothing saleable. Nothing great—
Just a joy 'cause I create,
While my teeth are getting clean,
Tales and poems which may be seen.

ONCE UPON A POEM

Mary lived in a one room flat,
With her rag doll and her cat.
Every morning off to work,
Beside Sam, the soda jerk.

She'd take cash. He'd scoop ice cream,
Unaware of Mary's dream,
That one day they'd fall in love—
Offer vows to heaven above.

But—alas—along came Suzy,
Making Sam light-headed and woozy.
In a month those two were wed.

Mary threw rice; no tear she shed,
'Cause at the wedding,
She met tall Fred.

And they became next item in town.
Catered affair in tux and gown.

So, dear Reader, you can see,
Mary and Ted lived in wedded glory—
Adding to another "happily ever" story.

CHILDHOOD

We were three in the neighborhood,
Playing as all children would,
Hide'n'seek and jumping rope,
Winning was our greatest hope.

Then one died. One moved away.
Loneliness was now my play.
Mom said, "Go to the library.
And there a new world you will see."
Vistas I had never known
Opened for me close to home.
Tales of fairies, elves and kings,
Magic cloaks, enchanted rings.

But alas, now I am grown
And the chores at work and home
Leave me little reading time,
And even less for this short rhyme.

AUTOBIOGRAPHY

When I was young I was free of care.
There seemed no worries anywhere.
My parents loved and I could tell,
How they made sure that my days went well.

Life was like a magic spell.
I had my share of things to do,
But school was first. I knew that too.

There was study time and play with friends,
School trips to planetarium and zoo,
I remember some. I forget some, too.

So much to learn at every turn.
Like days at beach, too much sunburn;
Dashing over the burning sand;
Into the water, holding mommy's hand.

Having few cares, I understand,
My mom and poppa guided me,
To be a dutiful child, you see.

To study for my tests at school—
Not studying would make me a fool.
So I obeyed my parents' wishes;
Studied, helped dust and wash the dishes.
Even fed our few goldfishes!

THE BEE

I hope that I will never see,
A bee in close proximity.
"Oh, Bee, as you fly in sun and shower,
    Don't ever mistake me for a flower."

CREATIVE WRITING

Words of water, words of fire,
　　Words of logic or desire,
　　Flowing from a poets' brain,
　　Easily—or with great pain,
　　Pour like songs out of the heart,
　　Burst life's silences apart.
Create worlds of darkest night,
　　Create worlds of sunlight bright.
　　Carry Man to heights unbound,
　　Reaching galaxies unfound,
　　In a burst of splendid phrase,
Writers create other time,
　　In their phrases or their rhyme,
Out of writings' difficult arts,
　　Men work with their broken hearts,
　　Rhyming, phrasing, weaving tales.
But the publisher rarely fails,
　　When accepting what men say.
　　They may publish,
　　But won't pay!

HOLIDAYS TODAY

The children were with us,
When we were all young;
Joining in songs,
We had always sung.

They carried the years,
Like melting snow,
Out of our house,
When they chose to go.

Our mirrors are frozen,
In splinters of scenes
Stirred up by photos,
And unbidden dreams.

The table is empty,
Snuff candlelight;
Festivities ended.
Prepare for the night....

CLOUD PICTURES

Here I lie in the sun-warmed grass,
Watching the clouds as they change and pass.
As the wind blows its way capriciously,
Cloud formations show their faces to me.
Here's a bird and there's a bat,
Or else a tree,
Or else a cat.
A movie show is there for me,
The audience upon the ground to see;
A movie film without a sound,
The willful breeze,
My sight does please.
I'd like some of the scenes to freeze,
But wind won't grant this wish of mine,
Following orders that are divine.
And soon the pictures in the sky,
Will disburse and shred and forever die.

THE SNOWS OF YESTERYEAR

This is a perfumed day today.
The breezes are in gentle play.
A butterfly kissed a rose on my bush,
And my heart stopped beating,
And life seemed hushed.

Up north there is ice and sleet and snow,
But our Florida weather makes flowers grow.
In my youth sleigh riding was my childish pleasure,
'Till shoveling walks became a chore beyond measure.
The warmth of Florida I cherish today,
Makes easy forgetting I wished snow would stay.
Still, memories return to the childhood pleasures,
Remembering those snowfalls as winter treasures.
Today I would not wish back those days—
Age turns the chapters of life other ways.
Picture postcards of new fallen snows,
Are all of winter times that I chose.
I'll write of winters I knew in December—
But need sunny days as I grow nearer to September.

The Inky-Dink

He was king of the forest, or so he said.
Right of succession—all family dead.
He was big as an eagle, but feathered all black.
Hard to spot him at nighttime,
But who'd want to keep track?
He wished he had relatives—
Others of his kind,
But nature apparently had no such thing in mind.
He met other creatures and one said that he
Should go off to other territories and seek out a She.
He thought it a good thing, that he should endeavor,
After all, he was handsome and extremely clever.
So off he went flying, over desert and mount;
But no other like him did he encount.
And just as he sadly turned back from his flight,
Daylight brought sunshine and much better sight.
And there in the sky, with wings gracefully applied,
Another bird like him he astonishingly spied.
With a flip of his wings, he dived to fly beside her.
How beautiful she was, was how he described her.
She led him to a rocky ledge; watched while he
Built them a nesting place for family to be.
And after a while they two became three,
And then four and more their family grew.
And now in the sky you can watch the while crew.

SPRINGTIME

Like sudden flames, the rosebuds burst,
Opening hearts as though in thirst.
Lilac bushes hug the wall,
Their violet petals blow and fall.

And white dogwoods carpet all the ground;
And breezes blow the petals around.
Oh spring! Your beauty takes my breath,
Seeing life return, after winter's death.

UNREQUITED LOVE

No, don't think that I am not aware,
How you glance my way through your auburn hair.
Do you think that I don't see you smile,
While your hand is in his, holding tight all the while!
I know you see my envy shine,
Knowing I think you are divine—
Wishing secretly that you were mine.
But you play me like a fish on a hook,
Smiling when you think I don't look.
Even though I turn away,
I'd embrace you—but I've feet of clay.
And so I know that he will win,
Because it is my biggest sin,
That I cannot tell you true,
How deeply is my love for you.
I'm a fool for the silence that I keep,
But only when awake, not when I sleep.
In dreams I pour my heart out to you.
In dreams I say I love you true.
In dreams my words are silver with love,
But when awake, you are too far above.
So, on the day when you are wed,
I will weep and wish that I were dead.
Others will whisper, "Silence was his evil brother—
So he must turn his back as she weds another!"

ALONE

You had no right to go away,
And leave me all alone.
No letters will you send to me,
Or call me on the phone.
It's hard for me to go to bed,
Expecting you to stroke my head.
I can't forgive that you are dead,
Despite our vows which you had said,
'Till death does sunder us apart."
I am alone, with a broken heart.

WHO IS THERE?

"Who is there?" he called aloud,
As he heard a knocking at the door.
No one answered as they hadn't answered,
Many times before.
"Stop playing tricks," he cried aloud,
Thinking it must be kids from down the street,
Supposing that their teasing was neat.
But he didn't think it was funny at all;
And took out a broom from the closet in the hall,
Planning to use the broom as a weapon—
Not menacing weaponry,
Not the kind to be real scary,
Not frightening, as he'd like it to be.
Still it was the best he had at hand,
And he would use it to make a stand.
"If you don't stop I'll make you sorry!"
He hoped his threat would make them worry.
But it was he who worried more,
For Death was waiting as he opened the door.

OBEDIENCE

How quiet the streets at twilight,
When folks are homeward bound from work.
But children still want playtime,
And homework they will shirk.
"Oh, Henry, I have called you a dozen times or more.
"I need you to pick some things up at the corner grocery store."
"I just have two more boxes to hop,
"And then I'll win the game.
"And then I'll run the errands.
"I promise, in God's name."
Mom said, "I don't like swearing.
"Be careful what you say.
"When your dad returns and I tell him,
"You'll sadly have to pay."
"Gee, mom, I never meant to hurt your feelings—not at all.
"And you've got my word,
I promise I'll come quickly when you call"
And that is how obedience is taught by mother to child.
Or laxness will assuredly drive poor parents wild.

THE TOY

The Ting-a-Ling was quite a thing,
Not human, or bird who liked to sing;
Invented in a toyland shop,
He had long legs on which he'd hop.

He wheeled along, or went kerplop.
If wound up he would rarely stop.
The parents of the little boy,
Bought Ting-a-Ling as their son's toy.

It gave the child much weeks of joy,
Till carelessly the child broke the toy.
Now Ting-a-ling's in the garbage bin.
But that's the way toyland has been,

And another toy replaces him.

JUMP FROG

Jump Frog believed he'd never fail
To be the Prince of fairy tale.
For ages, legends of his clan,
Said frogs had sometimes turned to Man.

But, somehow his ambition missed—
No girl he'd find who would be kissed.
"Me? Kiss a frog? Are you for real?
Your slimy skin holds no appeal.
I just might kiss my cat or dog,
But never kiss an oozy frog."

So, through poor Jump Frog's life was long,
He never changed into the song
Of Frog to Prince;
Just stayed until the end of days
A frog—no prince—a frog always.

MY CAT

My cat's a fastidious creature,
And most loving whenever she meets ya;
But I can't ever seem to quite teach 'er,
Why it makes me so miffed
When she brings me a gift,
Of some hunted-down, half-eaten creature.

TOM AND THE GENIE

"Grant me a favor," the old peddler said,
As the genie came out of the bottle.
"My Master, I can grant more wishes than one."
"Would three be alright, or a little?"
"Three I can handle," the genie advised;
"Just remember to give them some thought.
"Don't be nervous and spoil the whole deal,
Being hasty, or too overwrought."
The advice was quite wise, so Tom said,
"Keep me calm.
I want wealth, also love." He considered some more.
But the genie reminded, "I can grant you just three but not four.
Your wishes have now become your fate.
Here is the gold for your estate;
And love in abundance from your mourners,
Who see you as forever calmed.
Rest in peace in your grave—
You're embalmed!"

NOT A LENDER NOR A BORROWER BE

Like it or not,
There is a lot,
That one can say for living.
Give love for love;
Be tolerant;
With foes do be forgiving.
If you lend money to a friend,
And the friend cannot return it—
Smile quietly and say you'll wait,
And hope he soon will earn it.
But, if he does not soon repay,
And requests a time extension,
Be courteous and wait some more—
And when you meet, just mention,
"I hope you're planning to repay
The money that I lent you."
And if he says, "It's in the mail
That I already sent you."
Look in the box that day and next,
And in the days that follow.
Don't let yourself in anger,
Alternatively, self-pity, start to wallow.
Just hire a hit man of great skill,
In addition, pay him to collect the bill.
It won't take long until you're repaid,
And turn your days to golden,
Until the hit man lets you know,
You're eternally beholden.

BALLERINA

At night I hear music that comes in a dream;
The sweetness of players that never are seen.

I am one ballerina, in gossamer dressed,
Dancing sprightly along with the best of the best.

My elegant mask of feather and sequin,
Flashes a trail of where I have been.

Sparks from the lights of the orchestra pit,
Keep faceless the watchers wherever they sit.

Dark on the stage and dark in the house seats,
Rustling of paper, but no sound of heartbeats.

Yet the hall is filled to its full capacity,
As I dance with excitement at my own audacity.

I am light. I am graceful. I am all I can dream,
And the audience claps for me and my team.

They don't know, don't suspect,
That my steps are correct,

Not because I'm experienced in dancing the scene,
But because every movement is just part of a dream.

THE PRINCESS AND THE WITCH

In the jelly time of season,
When preserves were stored against freezin'
And the windstorms were all gone,
A fair princess babe was born.

While the townsfolk work and gaily sing,
"How beautiful seems everything!"
Unhappily there was a sting.
The baby put to sleep at night,
Was gone next morning—out of sight.

Her parents cried out in great fright,
And gloom reigned all the day and night.
Upon her broom a witch did ride,
With sleeping baby by her side;

And in a tower did they abide.
Too high, though princes often tried,
They could not claim their princess bride,

And Butterfly, which was her name,
Felt that the witch was all to blame,
For keeping her locked far away,
From mortals, where she'd rather stay.

But since the witch was the only one she knew,
Butterfly was often lonely and blue.
This put her into quite a stew,
Which could happen to me and happen to you.

Then one day while the witch was asleep,
The princess took the broom from her keep.

She sat on it, sideways astride,
And out of the tall tower she did glide.

She flew over towns, as an expert would ride,
Till down below where a horseman did ride,
She plunged, like an expert to stop at his side,
And ask if he'd consider making her his fair bride.

So divine a figure, so lovely a face,
To turn down such an offer would be a disgrace.
They found a preacher and quickly were wed.
When the witch found out she simply dropped dead.
So true love wins out, as is usually said.

IN THE FALL

Light green cabbage,
Tomatoes red.
The garden's colors,
Overbled.

The leaves on trees are turning, turning,
Till all the buses blaze like burning
And the cool winds set the crisp leaves scrunching;
Where footsteps crushed them in their bunching.

Evergreens stand, spiked and verdant,
Hollies with red berries burdened.
Cold winds flush the cheeks and face,
Make us walk a faster pace.

Hurriedly, you do aspire,
To sit before a warming fire;
Or look out through your windowpane.
From the warmth of your room you do admire,
The bushes that burn
But not with fire.

ON STAGE

When I was young, I played with dolls,
And pushed them in their buggies.
I'd pick them up and change their clothes,
And stop to give them huggies.

Then I grew up and met a man
I chose that I would marry.
We wed and as the years went by,
Three children I did carry.

There was a lot of happiness,
And sometimes there was strife.
But arguments along with joy,
Are all a part of life.

Now with the children all grown up,
And making their own way,
I live alone in a five-room house,
Where my children used to play.

They stay in touch by telephone,
And cards and letters I receive.
Their visits are a happy time,
And I hate to see them leave.

Still, I would like to journey back
To my happy childhood days;
But the curtain's down,
And will never rise,
On those past scenes on my stage.

ONCE I KNEW LOVE

Once I knew love when I was young.
And I spoke in an altogether different tongue.
I wrote in poetry.
In verses I'd rhyme.
Thoughts of love came to me most of the time.

I was romantic—or maybe love sick.
Poetry books I would mostly pick.
The jingles would jangle—some silly, some gay.
It seemed I could rhyme away all of the day.

Now I find myself not alone
Since an editor bought my little poem
And once there is talent,
It can show up again;
So let in the sunshine. And forget the rain.

IN THE DARK

After mommy died, then daddy said:
"Sarah, it is time for bed."
She washed her face and hands,
And on her knees her prayers she said.

Then daddy came and tucked her in,
And turned the night light off.
"Daddy," Sarah called in fear,
"Please leave the night light on in here."

"You silly girl," he scolded her,
"You're five years old, you know,
Too big to sleep with lights aglow."

"But daddy, I'm afraid at night,
And need the glow of my night light."
"There's nothing that you need to fear,
My own bedroom is very near."

"There's things that come here in the night,
And leave me shivering with fright."
"It's only in your mind, you know!"
"Please, daddy, leave my light aglow."

But daddy said, "Your fears are just inside your head."
He closed her door and went to bed.
She pulled her covers over her head,
So not to see the crawly things,

The ugly flyers with long stings;
But felt them all around her bed.

When daylight came to stop her dread,
Alas, alas, the child was dead.

FRIENDSHIP'S LOSS

My friends are going very fast;
I never thought I'd be the last.

I'm friendly, so I make new friends;
A nice beginning when another ends.
And yet, it isn't just the same,
New people always change the game.

It isn't easy to explain,
When friends have died there's always pain,
And life is changed for me again.

STORMS

If the wind blows strong,
They say beware.
Storms can cause us all a scare.
The hurricanes they track at sea,
May threaten you. May threaten me.

We watch the warnings on TV.
Hoping storms blow out to sea.
But, when they bring their winds and rain,
Life as we know it isn't the same.

Rainy days seem to be tame,
Compared to the gusts of the hurricane.
I wish that I may never see,
A hurricane in all fury.

We've had more than our share appear.
Please don't come back again this year.
In fact don't come back ever again;
We've had our fill of wind and rain.

And God, in your infinite wisdom, please—
Replace all hurricanes with just a strong breeze.

I WOKE IN THE MORNING

I woke in the morning to a bright new day;
At least on my wakening it seemed that way.

I opened the blinds, but the sky was gray.
Did this forebode a darker day?

No. Just let me smile and think happy thoughts:
Concerts and movies and brisk, healthy walks.

What if the sky is darker today?
Shall I spend time wishing a brighter new day?

For the time I've been given,
Let me just enjoy livin';

And wish for good health,
That's the best kind of wealth.

And—when I pass away,
Hope those who knew me best will say:

We will miss a good friend,
Who loved us 'til the end.

THE MARRY WIDOW

Etta had been married twice. Both her husbands had died tragically. Now my brother Doug wanted to marry her and even though Etta was my best friend, I found myself thinking superstitiously that marriage to Etta did not bode well for any bridegroom's longevity. Oh, I don't mean anybody suspected foul play on Etta's part—but it sure did seem like big coincidences that each husband died, leaving Etta very well endowed. And Etta was certainly well endowed by nature.

Her first husband Clay had fought successfully for her hand when she was eighteen, with hair like spun sugar and big, deep blue eyes. She was small-boned, but all the right places were softly rounded. She made a perfectly beautiful, storybook bride and when she threw the bouquet, I—her maid of honor—caught it. But I never caught a husband to fulfill the bouquet's promise.

As my dad always said, "Maggie, you're just too much heart-and-soul into our business. You think like a man. You outwork any man in the place. You ought to dress and act more ladylike After all, you do want a husband and children one day."

"No, dad. I like running the store with you."

"Well, I must confess, you're my right hand 'man'. Doug doesn't show any interest in anything but buying, fixing and racing cars. Sometimes I don't think he's got a head—either it's under a car hood, or under the car—with his feet sticking out."

Dad was right. Doug loved cars and I loved our department store where you could buy anything from prescriptions to appliances. Dad's father had started it at the turn of the century, a general store that grew into a million-dollar business.

Since Doug was two years older than I was—and a son—dad had tried to interest him in "coming in" as a junior partner. Doug resisted, so dad put him on a very generous allowance, so he could continue to pursue his hobbies, while I worked along with dad. I had just turned thirty when dad suffered a massive stroke and died.

I slipped easily into the company's presidency, with Doug in my care—as he had been since mom had passed away—when he was fifteen and I was thirteen. Maybe because I had mothered Doug all along, I was taken aback when he announced his intention to marry Etta.

I cried, "Doug, you said you never could stand Etta. You said she was a bore and wondered what I saw in her as a friend. You were probably the only male who didn't chase her. What made you change?"

"Well, you know she's had a lot of hard luck—two husbands dying so early in life. It left her depressed. When you insisted I go to her house with foods and flowers because you were too busy working to get there yourself, she was so 'down' I began to feel sorry and to try to kid around to make her perk up. I'd take her to a movie, or for ice cream and that lifted her spirits so much I'd get a kick out of thinking up ways to get her to smile and laugh again. I got especially interested when it thrilled her to go speeding in my car. Sis, it was because of you that I got to know Etta, then to like her, then to love her."

I had to agree that it was easy to love Etta. She was a perfect lady—she kept her house bright and spotless; she was a wonderful cook and host. She even coaxed lovely flowers out of her garden.

Her marriage to Clay had lasted seven long, happy years. We held them up as the model of a couple. Then Clay was walking across the road from his service and gas station to Diggs' Diner for his usual coffee break when some crazy hit-and-run driver barreled down the road and killed him—like the snap of a finger.

Etta—no great businesswoman—put the service station up for sale. She got a good price for it and since Clay had an insurance policy of $300,000, she was well set financially. But she just could not get over mourning for him.

The men of our town did not let her mourn for very long. They came to console her—or so they said—but it took less than a year for Andy Dunn to press her into another 'go' at marriage. And again, there followed the most perfect marriage you could want.

Andy built a house on a hill and there were always guests at the lawn parties. In winter there were steak dinners served around the big, dining room table, while a log-burning fireplace made everything extra cheery. Summers there were bar-b-ques on grills set near the heated outdoor swimming pool. Etta usually sat at the shallow side, dipping in her dainty toes and looking gorgeous in her French bathing suits. Andy dived and cut through the water, swimming right to Etta to catch a quick kiss and then swam back across the pool for another dive. That's what made it all the more tragic when Etta had to fly to Tucson, Arizona, to visit her widowed sister who was not well, having suffered for years with asthma. Before Etta left, she arranged to have the pool cleaned while she was away. The handymen drained the pool that very afternoon.

Andy, staying late at work because there was nothing to rush home to while Etta was out of town, came home close to midnight. He decided on a dip before going to sleep—not an unusual thing for him to do. His headlong dive into the pool he had not realized had been emptied, killed him instantly. It was not until the workmen came the next morning that they found his body.

Etta was inconsolable. She was filled with guilt. She would have had the pool torn down at once, but we, her friends, talked her into selling the property, pool and all and moving into a new condo in town to get away from the tragic memories of that house.

Poor Etta. Widowed again and barely thirty.

Everyone tut-tutted. She had to go through the dismal business of again selling her husband's successful business—the big hardware store on Main Street. The sale of the house and business netted her a financial windfall. Andy had not left any life insurance money because he felt that carrying insurance jinxed a man. Well, something had jinxed him and it was not life insurance. But Etta never needed that additional insurance money because she was a very rich widow after the demise of both husbands and the sale of their properties.

When Doug talked her into marriage some months later, I gave him away with much trepidation. I just could not shake the feeling that marriage to Etta was unlucky. But married they got and moved into the big mansion-type house down the street from me. Doug had been accustomed to living in a private house and felt they should live in "their" house, not "her" apartment.

Even after they moved in, Doug never did give up his room in the house where he had lived all his life. On those occasions when Etta visited her sister—perhaps once in three months—Doug stayed with me, still puttering and tinkering with the cars he kept in our garage.

The day that Etta got a telephone call that her sister was hospitalized again with asthma, Doug drove her to the airport, then came to our house so we could have supper together and he would stay until Etta's return.

Doug was not into cooking, but always prepared a cocktail for each of us. I had the chops and vegetables done, as he liked them. By the time we reached coffee, I found myself yawning.

"You've had a big day at the office. I'll do the dishes," Doug offered. That had been a standing joke with us ever since our dishwasher had been installed. I grinned and said I could manage and went into the kitchen. Putting my foot on the garbage can pedal I was in the process of shoveling the scraps out of the plates when a small, dark bottle caught my eye. In curiosity I fished it out, glancing at the label. It was a rather potent sleeping liquid from our pharmaceutical counter. "Now who would be taking this?" I wondered out loud, just as footsteps told me Doug was behind me.

"Did you finish the cocktail I made for you?" he asked as I turned, bottle in hand. His face was somewhat indistinct. But something in his question alarmed me. Some seventh sense caused me to cry, "You drugged me! Why?"

"To get the business."

The candid way he answered chilled me.

"But dad offered it to you." I could make no sense out of Doug and half expected him to grin and admit he was teasing. But he was perfectly serious—and truthful, "I don't want to work in the business. I want to get it for nothing—and sell it. I was inspired by the way Etta inherited her husbands' businesses, sold them and became wealthy. Didn't lift a finger. And that's how I want it. I'm no business man. Why work when I can inherit? No one will be surprised when I sell out after your death."

"… Your death…." The ominous words came to my ears as though from a long distance. Dismayed and helpless, I realized I was fast losing consciousness.

Doug lifted me and carried me upstairs to my bedroom. He laid me down on the pillow. He lifted my second pillow, preparing to put it over my face as soon as I was "out".

"Sorry, Sis," he really was apologetic. "I didn't want you to be aware that you had to die, but you won't feel anything once you're asleep. Tomorrow morning I'll call the police and tell them I couldn't awaken you. Your death will look like heart failure. After all, folks always said you'll kill yourself with work. Even an autopsy won't cause suspicion because many insomniacs take something."

"What about Etta?" I moaned.

"Oh, she'll be next. I'll think of some way. After all, you know I never cared too much for her…."

The pillow was descending. Just as I began to "black out" I heard a sound—as though a shot rang out. My last conscious thought was "Is he smothering and shooting me?"

Etta's worried face was bending over me. Behind her I saw the sheriff and uniformed deputies. As I struggled to sit up, Etta's arm was there to help me. The coroner's crew had marked in chalk an outline of a man's body on the carpet beside my bed.

Apologetically, the sheriff explained. "We had to shoot quickly, from the door. Your brother wouldn't lift the pillow from your face when we yelled to him. We're sorry, but it was his life or yours."

I heard my voice whisper, "How did you know?"

Etta said: "You can't be married to men without understanding them. Doug was always bringing up the subject of my husbands' accidents and how fortunate that it made me wealthy. He even, laughingly, mentioned how much wealthier we would be if you had an accident."

The sheriff told me, "You're lucky your sister-in-law put two and two together and came to us."

She supplied the additional information, "When I was packing my valise I saw Doug in the bureau mirror. He was reading directions on a vial which he slipped into his pocket. The strange smile on his face alarmed me so much that when he drove me to the airport I felt the need to say to him. "Look after Maggie. She works too hard. Make sure she's all right."

"Why?" he asked. "Wouldn't we be better off without her—like you are without Clay and Andy?" That sent such a chilling premonition through me that when he left me at the airport. I phoned my sister that I couldn't come that day. I canceled my flight and took a cab right to the sheriff's office."

The sheriff nodded, "What she said made us come right to this house. We rang the bell, but no one answered, so I shot the bolt and we ran upstairs. We were just in time to save you."

I felt such a well of gratitude that I burst into tears. "Thank you, oh, thank you." She really was my best friend. Then a thought struck me. "Oh, Etta, I am so sorry." This is your third husband to meet a tragic death." I looked into those beautiful blue eyes and realized, it won't be long before husband number four comes to court my friend Etta.

She realized that, too, but there was serenity in her eyes. She obviously had no fears about her next marriage.

"It will be all right," she assured me. "Bad luck only comes in threes."

THE SKY IS FALLING

When Valerie was a child she had heard the story of the animals who believed the sky was falling. She knew it was a fairy tale, but now she was sixty-three years old and knew the sky really falls.

Last year she and Don had retired and moved from Queens, to Orlando. The Starlite Development was everything they had dreamed. The money they had received from the sale of their Queens home paid for a two-bedroom, two-bath and zero lot-line house, large enough for their requirements because their forty years of marriage had been childless.

The first year they fixed up the house, did their own painting, wall-papering and landscaping. By year end they were amazed at how much they had accomplished. Don liked to do outside work while it was early morning and still cool.

He was digging a bed for a new hibiscus, when he fell forward on the earth. He must have made some sound because Val, mulching around the sago palm tree, spun around. With fear clutching her heart, she ran to him, calling his name. He never responded. He'd had a massive coronary and was gone in that short space of time.

Not only did the sky fall, but raindrops kept falling on Val's head. The months that followed were nightmares of grief and adjustment. She had to shoulder all the work she usually did and also learn Don's part of responsibilities, such as paying the bills, balancing the check book, sorting through his papers, his possessions, his clothes....

One morning Val walked to her next door neighbor's house and rang the bell. Zelda, a pleasant looking lady with short, salt-and-pepper hair, came to the door, wiping her hands on a paper towel.

Smiling at Val, she invited, "Come on in and sit down. I just baked blueberry muffins. Let's have coffee." Zelda's welcome was almost automatic. All the neighbors in the cul-de-sac were just as warmly hospitable. They had all moved here from out-of-town, far from old friends and family and the new life required that they extend themselves to those around them. It was an unwritten part of their life to care and be cared for. Yet, they did not intrude on their neighbors. But today Val had not come for a chatty visit. She came right to the point: "I need to get a driver's handbook at the Motor Vehicle Bureau."

Zelda's husband Jim came into the kitchen just then. Helping himself to a warm muffin, he cocked his head at Val. "What's the matter? Getting tired of riding with us?" Val flushed, "Oh, no, everyone's been great, giving me lifts to the doctors, the malls, the supermarkets—but I feel I'm imposing."

"Imposing!" Zelda was indignant.

"Zelda, it's true that I'm scared to death of driving and never had to do it in Queens where everything was within walking distance. But things are different here. Our Toyota Camry's only two years old, in good condition and staying in the garage, unused. Please Jim, help me once more. Get me the driver's handbook."

By late afternoon Jim brought the handbook to her. Sheer panic overwhelmed Val as she took it. But—frightening as it was—Val knew she must go through with this. She spent the next two days, studying the rules and regulations. At the end of that time she had practically memorized every printed page.

Jim drove her to the Motor Vehicle Bureau and then sat in the waiting room while Val was called to the testing area.

A perky, dark-haired girl with a reassuring smile, called her to the long counter where examiners were questioning applicants. Val handed over her Social Security card, her birth and marriage certificates and, when all the data was recorded, her examiner directed Val. "Look through this machine and read the eye chart."

Since Val used glasses only for close reading, she passed the standard vision screening and was assigned to one of the computers behind her. The instructions were on the screen. Her testing had begun.

She was directed to look at 20 road signs of various colors and shapes and tell their meaning. "This is fun," she thought as she breezed along, identifying each sign. Suddenly, a crossing gate flashed on and Val felt her heart freeze. What was it? She stared, concentrating. Almost ready to take a wild guess, she suddenly remembered and triumphantly punched the button identifying railroad crossing.

"Correct," the machine verified and Val felt the elation of obtaining 100% on the test. The road rules test was more tricky. Multiple answers were listed from which to choose and she made two incorrect guesses before she finished and the machine congratulated her on passing.

Awarded her learner's permit, she talked incessantly to Jim on the way home, needing to relieve the tension of test taking. "Now," she told him as he pulled up at her door, "comes the hard part—learning how to drive."

Leafing through the telephone book, she spotted an ad for an instructor. It seemed directed to her because it claimed, "special attention to the nervous."

Her instructor, Ben Marks, was a gray-haired gentleman whose erect posture came from Marine Corps training. He was a retired accountant who became a driving instructor five years ago after the death of his wife made it necessary to fill in the time. He told her all that as they drove around her neighborhood in his dual-control car.

He put Val at ease by quietly directing her to the mechanics of the car and the conditions of the road. "Look as far ahead as possible," he said. "Your peripheral vision will allow you to see what's around you."

He gave her three half-hour lessons a week. During those sessions Val was so tense, Ben had to ease her fingers off the steering wheel.

Jim and two of the other neighbors offered to practice-drive with her in her own car, but the thought of not driving in a dual-control car filled her with apprehension. Ben—very understanding and sympathetic—talked as they drove. She found her tension slipping away as she listened to him reminisce and she relaxed as she told him about those lonely days and nights after Don died. He was easy to talk to and interested in everything she said.

After the fourth lesson, Ben said, "I'd like to take you out to lunch. You could use the relaxation and I could use the company." Go out with a man? Val had not even considered such a thing. Wouldn't that be disloyal to Don?

As though he sensed her thoughts, Ben explained, "Believe it or not, Val, you are the first woman I've asked out since Julie passed away." They lunched at the Perkins Restaurant, in a booth with a window. Both ordered turkey on rye, with iced tea; they were pleasantly surprised that they followed similar diets. They discovered the same thing when they had dinner—two nights later—at a popular steakhouse.

When she made the appointment to take her driver's test, she felt more at ease, but when the test was over and she had failed, all the apprehension returned.

"He tricked me," Val sobbed in the car, as the quiet Ben drove her home. "The examiner said, 'Park here' and when I reversed and bumped into something, he said, 'You hit a fire hydrant.' I jumped out of the car to look and sure enough there was a small hydrant in the midst of high bushes. I got so angry, I yelled, 'You made me do an illegal park. You're supposed to be legal.' He failed me quickly and said, 'Drive back.' I think he was afraid I would hit him with my purse."

"Would you have?" Ben asked quizzically.

"No, I would have used the tire iron in the trunk."

Ben put his head back and laughed. Val, still teary-eyed regarded him and then, despite herself, began to smile. In a little while, they were laughing together. Once again, he had eased her tensions.

He would not accept money for the next two weeks of lessons. "I can't be paid by someone I plan to marry," he said. He put his hand over hers, as they clutched the wheel tightly; at his touch, she felt her grip relax.

It was no longer teacher-to-pupil after that. It was heart-friend to heart-friend. And when Val took her next test, she passed and came out in triumph, holding up her driver's license—photo and all.

Smiling, Ben slid from the driver's side to the passenger side. Val got behind the wheel. He kissed her cheek. "Congratulations, future Mrs. Ben Marks," he said.

Val started the car.

Sometimes the sky falls and sometimes, when that happens, it scatters sunshine down.

THE WORTH OF A MAN

Ben Williams was not a doctor; but at Fry Creek everyone called him "Doc". In his drugstore at Cherry and Third, he dispensed prescriptions, sundry items and sound advice through the pharmaceutical window or over the counter.

Right now he was at a loss for consolations to offer the twelve-year old boy who stood tearful before him with a bloodied mouth and slightly swelling eye. "Matt Hogan's gang again?"

Roger Thayer nodded. "They caught me outside of school."

"That's the third time and the school term's just started. I'll speak to the principal."

"NO!" It was almost a shout. "They'd only make it worse for me. They'd call me a snitch, as well as a—a thief."

To give a kid a stigma because of something his father had done just made Ben's blood boil. He was especially furious because this was Mary's son—the son that might have been his—if Todd Thayer, despite Ben's patient courtship, hadn't swept Mary off her feet.

"Thief?" Ben's voice shook with indignation, "Why, you never stole anything in your life!"

"My father did, so everyone thinks, like father like son. But Matt Hogan's a fine one to call names! His father's punchy from all that boxing—but no one calls Matt punchy."

"Matt's no different than any of the other kids. They repeat what their folks say and they haven't got the brains of a microbe. To hound a boy because his father made a mistake!"

"Mistake?" Roger's laugh was bitter. "Some mistake—to steal money from the bank where he was the manager and try to run so they had to shoot him."

"Your father must have been sick, because he was a good man. It's just that he liked good times—and easy money—and let temptation get to him. It was just one bad slip...."

"... Which I have to pay for." Roger was a studious-looking boy with quiet gray eyes like his mom's and a lean, good-looking face; but now, his expression was resentful, "I wish we'd move out of this town."

Pity for the boy made Ben's heart ache. "Roger, you know your mother's reason for staying. Gossip has a way of finding you, wherever you are. You've got to win their respect."

"Win their respect! How am I supposed to do that?"

"Well, there are a couple of ways, but the best way would be to fight Matt Hogan. Win or lose, you'll prove you've got guts."

Roger looked at Ben as though he had gone crazy. "Fight Matt? Matt is three years older than me and fifty pounds heavier. He doesn't have to lift a finger; he could squash me just by knocking me down and jumping on me, or getting his arms around me and crushing me."

Ben came around the counter and put his hand on the boy's shoulder. "Listen, Roger, I used to train in the ring to keep myself in shape, so I know a bit about defense. Let's start some lessons right now, today. We can work out behind the store. It's a blind alley—no windows on the building next door—so no one can see. Okay?"

Roger was dubious. He had no hope of being able to challenge Matt successfully. But, not knowing any way out, he sighed, ready to try anything, no matter how hopeless.

Heeding Ben's last warning to stay out of Matt's way, Roger offered his homeroom teacher help with blackboard washing, freshening bulletin boards and other clean-up chores. In that way he was able to spend an extra half-hour in school, after dismissal.

Matt Hogan and his buddies were not inclined to hang around the school longer than necessary, so by the time Roger left the class and came into the schoolyard, it was empty.

For a month, Roger made his way from school to Ben's store. Joe Brown, Ben's clerk, took over while his boss trained Roger. The fall days were fair. Indian summer was hazy, but rainless—perfect weather for working out.

Ben mainly instructed Roger how to weave and dodge and look for an opening to connect with a punch. They did not wear gloves because Ben felt Roger had to become adept in street fighting, not a ring match. They knew that sooner or later Matt would find an opportunity to start tormenting Roger again. So, everyday that there was no encounter with Matt gave Roger more confidence in his ability to defend himself—and maybe even land some blows of his own.

"You don't have to be Matt's equal," Ben reminded Roger. "Bullies don't like to see their own blood. So, if you can manage to give him one good punch, you could surprise him enough to make him think twice about tackling you anymore. That's what we need to spar for. Don't be afraid of hitting me. Just keep weaving, to get out of the way of whatever I throw at you. Duck and dodge. But keep watching for that one opening when you can come in swinging—and when you do, swing as hard as you can."

One other bit of advice Ben gave Roger; "If Matt starts up with you, tell him you're ready to fight him." Roger looked skeptical. He was scared and said so.

But Ben assured him, "When you tell Matt you're ready to meet him, it will take him by surprise. Bullies don't expect their victims to stand up to them. It throws them off to think their opponent may be prepared—and unafraid."

"Unafraid! I'm scared to death."

"I know, but you've got some training on your side now. You're not totally defenseless like you were when school started. Just remember, when Matt starts up with you again, tell him you'll meet him." And Ben told Roger exactly what he was to say to Matt.

Two days later, Roger came out of school to find Matt and two of his cronies waiting on the corner for him.

Roger froze. They sauntered up to him. Matt grinned and got all set to start pushing Roger around when Roger looked him right in the face and said, "Listen, Matt. I'll fight you, if you want, but not here!"

Matt's mouth opened in surprise. Narrow-eyed he looked at him. "What do you mean not here!"

"I mean, if you want to fight, let's not do it near the school!"

"What are you talking about?"

"I'm talking about meeting after school tomorrow at the empty lot on Church and Middle Street. I'm ready to fight you there!"

Matt couldn't believe his ears. "You mean you're gonna take me on?" Roger nodded because he was too scared to speak.

Matt stared at him for a long, hard minute; then he grinned. "Sure," he agreed. "I can wait until tomorrow to knock your brains out. I ain't in no hurry at all. C'mon, fellas, tomorrow ain't far off." And laughing loudly, they turned and left.

At Ben's place Roger sparred furiously. Ben assured him that he'd learned a great deal in just a few weeks. And, as Roger danced nimbly around Ben, the latter kept urging, "Weave and dodge. And watch for an opening—to land a punch."

Roger didn't sleep well and his stomach fluttered all day in school. But when the three o'clock dismissal bell sounded, he excused himself promptly and doggedly went with three of his friends, to meet Matt at the vacant lot.

Matt and his gang were late. They felt there was no rush. "One sock," Matt promised, "and ole Rog won't ever take on anyone even an inch taller."

The lot was weed-grown and rose toward a hill where a house had once stood. It had burned and some of the seared timber still lay moldering about. A wide driveway, which had once led up to the entrance, had grass pushing through the cracked cement. Litter, rusted cans and torn papers blew about in the gentle wind.

Ben had left his store to go with Roger; he bent to whisper to him, "Remember about weaving and dodging and looking for an opening to hit him. Keep your back to the lot and make him face that direction, so the sun shines in his face."

Roger nodded and walked cautiously toward his opponent. Matt didn't wait for the usual "shake hands and square off." He fairly flew forward, fists swinging. Roger danced nimbly aside and the blows fell on empty air.

Matt looked surprised. A moment later he dove forward again. Roger moved aside. Matt's face became bellicose. He didn't rush in a third time. He kept his eyes on the smaller boy, his elbows close to his sides, his hands clenched murderously.

Roger never took his gaze off his face. He was grateful there was a breeze because, although it was a cool day, he was sweating. Matt's growing fury became more frightening. His face was turning red and Roger feared that if he worked himself up further, he would pulverize him.

Roger danced away, putting more distance between them. Matt's face got darker red. His eyes grew smaller. His features contorted. He rushed forward.

"Watch for the opening!" Ben cried.

Roger leapt in and with all his strength, hit Matt on the nose.

Bellowing, Matt staggered backward, touching his nose. His hand came back with blood. Matt stared—unbelieving—at his own blood. To the astonishment of the onlookers Matt's eyes filled with tears. In a rage, Matt rushed at the smaller boy. Even as he was moving, his head went up, his mouth opened and he began a spell of sneezing. Roger took one look at those eyes filled with tears and the head tilting back for another sneeze and he rushed in, right hand clenched.

As Matt's head came down to complete the sneeze, Roger connected with every bit of strength he could muster. Matt staggered back. Roger came in again. Another direct punch to the nose—and the big boy rocked where he stood, fell backward and hit the ground. His sprawl was ludicrous because his face was twisted into an unbelieving, totally astonished expression. He did not attempt to rise. He could not believe he had been knocked down and was lying at the feet of the boy who had accomplished this.

Roger bent down and extended his hand. Matt simply stared at him. His friends rushed over to help him up. He shook his head and waved them away. As they withdrew, Matt looked piercingly into Roger's eyes. Roger kept his hand extended. Slowly, grudgingly Matt reached out. Gripping hands, Roger pulled the other boy up. Towering over Roger, Matt looked down. Roger had all he could do to keep fear out of his face. Inwardly, he was churning. Would Matt belt him?

Surprisingly, Matt shook his hand. "I don't know how you did it, but you won—fair and square."

One of Matt's buddies growled something about a trick, but Matt shook his head.

"He did his best," he called over his shoulder, "and from now on we leave him alone." Turning to his friends, he said, "It's over. Let's get going."

When they left, Roger's friends crowded around to congratulate him. Ben grinned. Things had gone better than he had hoped. Roger had discovered that size didn't always make a winner or a loser. Ben had often told him, "The worth of a man depends on his own self-esteem." In fact, Ben realized, it was about time for him to become more than just a friend to Roger. He had put off his courtship of Mary for too long. It was time to prove his own worth.

There were certain advantages to being the only pharmacist in town. He knew all the ailments of the people. Matt, since boyhood, had been a hay-fever sufferer. Ben looked up at the empty lot where the wind blew the grasses and weeds. The spore count had been particularly high this week. The lacy white flowers of the Queen Anne's Lace were carried in the air. And, in thick clumps on their stalks, bowing their bright heads in the winds that carried their pollen were the wild and profusely growing goldenrods.

WILL GRANDMA COME HOME AGAIN?

The pre-holiday crowds in the airport terminal were feverish and noisy. Why then did the small boy's voice seem to rise above the din, stopping me in my tracks, frozen and dry-mouthed? He was just to the right and ahead of me, holding the hand of his mother.

"Mommy, if Grandma flies away to Aunt Helen, will she come home again?"

I saw the elderly woman who was walking toward the security table. When she turned and threw an anguished look at the boy and his mother, such a wave of deja vu swept over me that I had to back over to a wall to stop the trembling that filled my body, making my legs too unsteady to hold me.

The wall supported me, but I could see that the elderly woman had passed through security and the mother was turning away, towing her youngster toward the terminal exit. Her words did not reach me, but I could have mouthed them myself, "Of course Grandma will come back. She's only going on vacation for a few weeks." I could see the young woman's face and although there was relief mingled with some guilt, the guilt was much less and the relief was much greater.

I had the urge to reach out and touch her arm and draw her aside to say, "Don't let your mother go. I know that it means freedom for you and your husband. I know you'll be mistress in your own home. You won't need to feel guilty about going out in the evenings, or having to explain what you are cooking, or the way you are cooking. I know that's all very important. You need the kind of privacy you are going to get now. But don't extend it."

If I had put my arm out to the young woman—if I had said all those words—what would have been her reaction?

She would have looked at me. Maybe she would have said, frowning and icy, "I beg your pardon! I don't think this is any of your business." She would have pulled herself out of my grasp and gone off, hauling a rather perplexed child in her wake.

I visualized all this and it sent me back in time to such a moment when I had been in another airport, like this one and my little girl had asked the same question, "If Grandma flies away, will she come back home to us?"

"Of course."

I had been so sure. Mother had lived with my husband and myself since our marriage. It seemed natural at the time, to have my widowed mother—with whom I had lived all my life—move to the larger apartment when Joe and I got married. After all, he and I both worked. Mother had not worked since her own marriage. In those days, women became housewives at marriage and their husbands were the breadwinners. My father had been a steady breadwinner and my mother a frugal housekeeper. After he suddenly died of pneumonia one hard, bitter winter, there was very little life insurance. The savings they had dutifully put away was what tided us over until I finished commercial high school and got a job as stenographer in a law firm.

Mother wanted to earn her own living, but there were few opportunities for women without skills or experience. That did not seem to matter as long as my husband and I were working. Mother managed the house, the shopping and the cooking. She had supper waiting when we came home and breakfast ready in the morning. We weren't pressured with housework. And when we invited other couples over, Mother discreetly withdrew to her room, or went to a movie, or visited someone—even though we protested that she could "Stay. You're not in the way." But, in our hearts, we were glad that she did not give in to our protestations.

Our life might have gone on in this way, but it changed with the birth of our first child. Although Mother was invaluable during my inexperienced motherhood, I felt a growing resentment at not being in full control of my own baby. Perhaps if the apartment had been larger; perhaps if Mother had had hobbies, or places to go—it might have given us the privacy I began to crave in the rearing of my daughter and the managing of my household. Now that I was home, I wanted the kitchen to be my own, the baby to be my own and the time with Joe to be his and mine alone.

Mother was trying so hard to help, that I found myself becoming testy. "Why do you hover around?" I cried, "Don't you trust me to take care of the baby?"

The surprise, the hurt look, the inane, "I was only trying to help...." only added to my irritation. At night I'd pour all of this in Joe's ear, when we were in bed.

Joe had always loved Mom. He was such an easy-going man. If it bothered him that we were always a threesome, he did not complain, because that was what I wanted. Now suddenly, it was not what I wanted. Night after night, "Mom said this and Mom did this...." Joe—intensely loyal to me—ventured, "Maybe she should get her own apartment."

That stopped my tirade. Most of mom's insurance and savings had been used up in the years I trained for a job. Neither she, nor Joe and I, had enough money for two apartments. That solution was an impossibility. But mom's continued life with us was becoming more difficult. I was pregnant again. Another child in the apartment would need to relegate mom out of the bedroom and into the living room. With Joe being the only one earning a salary, we simply could not afford to move into a larger place.

With the arrival of the second baby, the crowding and stress became worse. Mom and I quarreled more often. We made up, but less often. There were tears, recriminations. I resolved to become more patient and she tried to slip further into the background, retiring earlier to her room, going more often to movies she may have seen before, or did not care to see at all.

Then came the letter from Mother's sister—my Aunt Judy in California. She invited Mother for a visit, even sent her a ticket. I suspected Mother may have written of the difficulties between us.

Mother showed us the letter at the supper table and looked into our faces, saying, "You do think I should go, don't you?"

I thought, fleetingly, "She wants us to say, 'No, don't go.'" It was only a momentary thought, quickly swept aside by relief.

"What a wonderful vacation that will be for you," I bubbled. "You've never really taken time off and this would not only be an exciting trip, but a great opportunity to see your sister. She's been in California for more than five years. You haven't seen her in all that time."

"No," Mother agreed faintly, "We haven't seen each other in a long time. I— I guess I should go" Anxiously she asked, "You're sure you won't be needing me? After all, the children are so young."

"Don't worry," I said it too quickly, "we'll manage just fine. Don't give us another thought. We'll be all right—really."

I know it wasn't what she wanted to hear, but the invitation from California was the answer to my prayer and I didn't want any doubts to stop it from coming to pass. If Mother would leave, I would be free—mistress of my house, my family.

In no time, Mother and I had shopped for "California" clothes, packed her suitcases, drove her to the airport and kissed and hugged her good-bye, waving frenetically, repeating, "Have a good time." We ignored the wistful look in her eyes, the faint, "You will let me know if you need me, won't you?"

When passengers boarding the plane hid her from our view, my daughter asked, almost tearfully, "Mommy, if Grandma goes away, will she come home to us?"

"Of course, darling," I assured her, "It's just a visit with her sister."

Mother's letters arrived from California. "I miss you all so much," she wrote in each one. "I can't wait to come home."

My letters said in return, "Take advantage. Stay as long as you can."

I never once wrote the words Mother wanted to hear, "We miss you, too. When are you coming home?"

Mother never did come home. Aunt Judy telephoned. She was crying so hard it was difficult to understand that Mother had died suddenly in her sleep. She would never see any of us again. And we would never see Mother again.

I had never thanked her for all the years of caring for us. She had made time to consider all of us and I had made no time to consider just her.

I hurried to board my plane, hoping to sit beside another Grandma going to "visit" her sister. Perhaps I would talk to her. Perhaps I would hold her hand. Perhaps I would say the words to her that I had meant to say to my mother. "You are needed. You will be missed. Your family loves you."

When I say this to someone else's mother, I am saying it to mine. "Mother, your family misses you. Your family loves you."

But Mother has gone to another home.

"Grandma won't come home to us—ever again."

IN LIMBO
(The story of an angel's revenge)

Shari was the only one who knew Bert had murdered her. It made her furious. Here she was, in limbo and unable to prove or avenge her murder. The problem was that, as long as no one was aware there had been a murder, Bert could never be brought to justice. And, as long as he was not brought to justice, Shari would have to remain in limbo and not ascend to the Higher Level.

What was even more infuriating was that Shari could not communicate with anyone. She had no inkling of how she knew about any of the rules. She didn't even know if they were called rules. Who made them up? She didn't know. How long had she been here? How long would she remain? She didn't know. She had no feeling of time passing or time existing. Things came to mind, which she knew were valid. She accepted them and realized that her main concern was to get out of limbo.

"That rotten Bert," she fumed. "Double-crossing husband. He's living high on the inheritance from my death and everyone's consoling him. Oh, wouldn't I like to burst his bubble!"

Shari was talking from past experience. In her present existence she was bodi-less—a wraith—floating in a fog-like, non-place.

She was a novice to this new form. She did not know what kind of skills she possessed. Would abilities come to her naturally? Would they need to be acquired? Learned? This uncertainty did nothing to ease her anger at Bert for causing her to be here.

She doubted that when Bert proposed marriage, he had it in mind to kill her for her money. She had been born an heiress, the only child of Mums and Daddy Fox of the nationwide Fox Floral Nurseries, well recognized by the logo of the sharp-nosed foxhead, sporting a flowery bonnet.

An angina problem at birth had always kept Shari in delicate health. A trained nurse lived in the big mansion especially to see to her needs. Private instructors came daily to tutor her, teach her dancing, piano, swimming. All had their appointed times and Shari had a full schedule. Because she was surrounded by people and because her doting parents made it their business to breakfast and supper with her, Shari never had a feeling of loneliness.

The doctors checked her condition regularly but, when she turned twenty, a change in her EKGs brought about a conference between her internist, cardiologist and neurologist. They concurred. Shari needed to start a regular regime of physical exercises. Mums and Daddy, who never deprived Shari of anything, hired a contractor to add a gym room to the west wing of the house which led to the swimming pool area.

They offered him the job of ordering the proper equipment and of becoming Shari's coach and the fitness instructor of the country club. The contractor had constructed a cottage adjoining the gym. So Bert moved into Shari's life.

Bert, at twenty-nine, was built like a Greek God, with a face to match. The day he was introduced to Shari she fell in love. It seemed miraculous that he was to be with her six days a week, to bring her to normal health through exercise and proper diet.

She was thrilled when his arms steadied her as he guided her on the exercise machines, or supervised her water aerobics. She found excuses to invite him dinner, which, heretofore, had been a strict threesome—her parents and herself.

Bert fit in as though he had been a son of the family. He was soft-spoken and charming. He was well read and able to hold his own in conversations that ranged from current topics to classics, or best-selling books. He had been raised in an orphanage and it was remarkable what discipline it had required to build up his body and mind.

One evening, the two of them were taking their usual after-dinner stroll in the garden. The fragrance of the hyacinths and roses filled the air. A full moon bathed them in the dappled shadows of the oleanders and chestnut branches and she was tinglingly aware of her slim hand in his firm clasp.

He stopped at the stone bench where they often rested because she could not sustain too prolonged a walk. He turned to her, looming tall and strong with the moonlight full on his face. His eyes and his voice were tender and he put his hands on her shoulders.

"Shari, honey, you must surely know how I feel about you." She nodded wordlessly. He could not have been insensitive to how his very nearness made her tingle.

It was a miracle when he said, "Shari, I love you. Will you marry me?"

She almost stopped breathing. She had to curb the impulse to throw her arms around him and cry, "Yes. Yes, my darling." But innate caution made her suppress her racing pulses and keep the excitement out of her voice. She finally managed to say, "Bert, I care for you very much, but I can't give you a definite answer yet."

He smiled, no way put out, "Of course you can't. I didn't really expect you to accept me right off the bat." He reached into his pocket and withdrew a small velvet box. He opened it and there in the satin lining was a small blue-white solitaire. "It isn't much," he said ruefully, "but I saved my salary to buy this for you. I'll put it on your finger the day you say, 'Yes' and we set the date."

She had all she could do not to cry impulsively, "Let's get married tomorrow." Returning to the house, she hurried to tell her parents. "I know," she ended, "that he wants to marry me for my money, but I don't care. I'm not so proud that I would turn down the one man I want just because I'm rich and he's poor."

Her parents agreed and promised to reward their prospective son-in-law for his good sense. After the honeymoon, they took Bert into the business as the junior partner, with a full contract and stock options and other perks.

The only stipulation in the contract was that all the benefits, including the job, would end if Bert ever wanted a divorce. Shari did not delude herself into believing that Bert could be faithful. Her physical condition did not permit the sort of sex that a man of Bert's strong appetites needed. She was tolerant of his affairs. They were brief. He always returned to her with his careful, tender lovemaking. She was content and he made it his business to keep her happy and in the best of health.

Their first years were idyllic. In the fourth year of their marriage, tragedy struck. On a business trip to determine if South American markets could be financially feasible, Shari's parents died in the crash of their private jet.

Shari collapsed. Bert stayed at her side, giving her total care and attention. His dedicated ministrations finally enabled her to make the transition from grief to acceptance.

The reading of the will was a formality. At the age of twenty-four Shari found herself chairman of the board of the multi-million dollar business. Wisely, her parents had set up a corporation composed of trusted executives who ran the enterprise as always.

Shari's life was little changed. However, their old faithful retainers were left such substantial incomes, that they could comfortably retire. Particularly set up for life was the housekeeping couple who had cared for the estate since Shari's birth. Their windfall enabled them to return to their Swedish homeland, to live out their lives in financial comfort.

They recommended that their twenty-six year old niece Inger take over the managing of the house. Inger had performed similar duties for the burgomaster of the town in which she had been born and raised. Inger turned out to be as efficient as her aunt and house affairs ran as smoothly as always.

Inger's capabilities were only outshone by her good looks. Slender and tall, with the lithe body of an athlete, she spent her free time doing exercises that kept her physically fit.

Sometimes when Shari looked out the window and saw Inger and Bert swimming in the pool together, she likened them to Aphrodite and Apollo. She never suspected that, like the Gods of Olympus, these two would become lovers. In all innocence, she believed in their loyal commitment to her comfort and well-being.

Inger took Shari in hand and turned Shari's mousy-brown ponytail into a shoulder-length, ash-blonde body-wave. Soft earth tones highlighted the planes of Shari's cheeks. Bert was enchanted by Shari's change from frail, colorless girl to pretty lady.

Then came the day Shari passed by the dining room window which looked out into the pool area. And, there were Apollo and Aphrodite in the water, arms about each other in a tight embrace, passionately kissing.

"Just a passing affair," Shari assured herself. But, watching the ardor of their lovemaking made it difficult to dismiss this as just a casual amour.

Becoming watchful, she took to creeping stealthily to places where she could remain hidden and observe them. Witnessing the intensity of their lovemaking from such secret hideouts as the tree-screened arbor, or the privacy of the gym cottage, Shari, in dismay, could not justify their trysts as passing dalliances. Bert's feelings seemed deeper than in any previous affair.

One day, at breakfast, in the sunny morning room, Shari told Bert, "I've come to a decision."

He laid aside his newspaper and gave her smiling attention. "What decision, honey?"

Her heart was pounding, fearful of his reaction, but doggedly determined, she plunged ahead, "I've decided to let Inger go."

"Go?" blankly, "Go where?"

"Back to Sweden. I'm giving her two weeks' notice and a substantial severance pay, along with a one-way plane ticket."

Utter disbelief was in his face. He was speechless.

Hastily, she explained, "I know you two have been having an affair. You've had other affairs. I never interfered because I realized they were just flirtations to you. But, with Inger, it's different. I'm afraid you're falling in love with her and will want to leave me."

Bewilderment played across his features. "Honey, I would never dream of leaving, or divorcing you. Inger is just another playmate. You are the only love of my life." He spoke so sincerely, Shari's heart was wrenched. Could she have been wrong? Could she have been over hasty? Abashed at the injustice she might have done Bert, she became apologetic.

"If I'm making a mistake and, if Inger is really just a passing fancy, it shouldn't upset you too much to have her leave. Truthfully, my darling, it would kill me to lose you."

He strode to her, drew her out of her chair, into his arms. "My foolish baby, how could you doubt me? You are my love. If it will prove this by sending Inger away, then that's what you must do." And when he kissed her and fire coursed through her body, she mentally berated herself for her doubts. Bert might stray for a while, but he would never make the mistake of choosing another woman.

"You know," he was so sincere, "in two weeks it will be our anniversary. Let's not spoil it with unpleasantness. I've already planned a dinner celebration here at home, early to bed and then, off on a cruise—just we two—for a week in the Caribbean. When we return you can replace anyone you choose. In the meantime, I will stay clear of Inger. How does that sound, darling?"

"Oh, Bert," she melted into his embrace. At their anniversary dinner, the candlelight shone on the keys he took out of the small, ribboned package she gave him. They were for her gift to him—a crimson Ferrari with cream colored, Italian leather upholstery.

He brought over a long white box tied in gold. When she opened it and removed the tissues, there was his gift to her—the finest shimmering satin designer nightgown with a matching peignoir so sheer and full that the lightest breeze caused it to float and the wide sleeves to spread like gossamer wings.

He lifted two champagne glasses and gave her one. "A toast," he proposed, "to the only love of my life."

He raised the glass to his lips, but she hesitated. "Bert," she whispered guiltily, "You know I can't drink. Liquor makes me sleepy...."

"Who's talking about liquor," he laughed. "This is champagne—just bubbly. You're entitled to it on our anniversary. Once a year can't do any harm." Abashed at her fears, she smiled tremulously, then clinked her glass against his and drank down the contents in one defiant gulp.

Almost immediately she felt the reaction. Her skin became flushed and her head felt heavy. She clung to him for support, murmuring, "Oh, Bert, I'm sorry to be such a baby, but I'm finding it hard to stand up."

"Then, I'll carry you," he said gallantly and scooping her up in his arms, strode up the circular hall steps, leading to their bedroom. Her drooping head rested on his shoulder. Contentedly she sighed as he laid her carefully down on the coverlets. "Oh, darling," she wailed with sudden remembrance, "My new nightgown. I must wear it tonight."

He grinned and hurried downstairs, to bring the gift and place it on the bed. "I must put it on. It's our special night," she murmured and fought against the drowsiness.

With effort she got off the bed, snatched the set from its protective tissues and, staggering slightly, headed for the bathroom to prepare for her anniversary night.

She barely made it back to bed where he had remained, standing, ready to assist her. All she had time to do was collapse amongst the satins. Then she was asleep.

With gentle solicitude he bent, straightening her limbs, smoothing the night-gown and peignoir about her, crossing her arms over her breast and tucking back stray tendrils of hair. With fond eyes he studied her, pleased that her sleep was so deep and peaceful. His affection was genuine as he bent to kiss her forehead and her lips. Then he lifted the pillow beside her and pressed it, firmly and inexorably, over her face.

Panic woke Shari to brief awareness. Her hands flailed out beseechingly. Her last conscious thought was the incredulous realization, "He really loves Inger—enough to murder for her!"

She had not expected that. But it was too late. Her senses spiraled away and darkness took over....

And now, in limbo, her mind was consumed with how to avenge Bert's treachery. She discovered how to will herself back to the scene of the crime. Without substance, she floated above the pool area, where Bert and Inger made love on the oversized pool cushions. The servants had been assigned outside errands. No one was about.

Bert untied Inger's halter, laying it at poolside.

With utmost concentration, Shari caused up a flurry of air that blew the halter into the pool. The lovers sat up, staring where the garment bobbed on inexplicable eddies.

"I'll get it," Bert volunteered, starting to rise. Inger pulled him back. "Later," she whispered.

Shari, with mighty determination, sent the water churning, in a waterspout, out of the pool, drenching them.

Wiping their eyes, they stared, stupefied at the pool. But Shari had desisted and all was calm once more. Bert looked up to see if there were any storm clouds, but the sky was blue and clear. With no evidence to explain the phenomenon, Bert rose, reached down to draw Inger to her feet. "Might as well go in," he decided and the two of them went into the cottage.

Shari, floating above, was filled with frustration. She had accomplished nothing, except one thing—the realization that Inger was innocent and did not even know murder had been done. It was Bert alone—the planner and the doer. Shari would have to rethink her strategy.

Shari experimented with thoughts that came to mind. She considered levitation, but sending objects across space did not offer any practical solution. Clanking chains would only bring in a plumber to inspect the pipes. When Shari finally hit upon a workable technique, it required utmost determination and willpower to perfect. Being an energy force, it could only last a few moments. So she had to make sure it succeeded in the time allotted.

Fox Floral Nurseries stretched over the south end of town. Verdant acres of plants, shrubs and trees sprawled amid roads and paths where buyers could walk or ride to select their purchases. Green houses abounded. The showrooms and corporate headquarters were in spacious white and glass enclosed structures with easy access from the parking lots. The railroad extended special spurs for refrigerated boxcars to bear fresh flowers out to the waiting markets.

Bert could easily have led the hedonistic life that had become his inheritance, but he was ambitious to become chairman of the board. With the firm resolve that helped raise him from an orphan to the heir-apparent of the nation's largest plant grower, he reported to work every day, like any dedicated employee; he wanted to earn the top position through his own efforts.

Shari counted on Bert's punctuality when she chose to put her plan into action.

As expected, he reached the railroad track heading to the nurseries just before the 8:00 a.m. train. He was accustomed to crossing the track and driving his Ferrari down the road leading straight to his reserved parking space in front of the glass doors of the executive offices.

His car was right on the tracks when he suddenly and violently jammed his foot full force on the brake and shrieked, "What's THAT??"

THAT was a white, shimmering form, materializing on the other side of the track, directly in the path of his car.

The thunderstruck man beheld the figure growing clearer and more defined. He thought his eyes were playing tricks. Was that really a woman appearing out of nowhere? He took one hand off the wheel to rub his eyes. Was he seeing things? Was he hallucinating?

The shape was becoming sharper—more familiar. Goggle-eyed he gasped, "Shari!"

There she was! Dressed as he had last seen her—in the nightgown, with the sheer peignoir billowing out and the sleeves fluttering like angel wings as her arms extended to either side.

Ear-splitting warning whistles sounded with frantic repetition from the approaching train. Vibrations from the speeding freight cars shook the rails beneath the car.

On the crossing gate, lights were flashing insistently!

The crossing gates came down in front and in back of the stopped Ferrari. Bert could easily have driven through had he not remained paralyzed at the wheel. Eyes bulging at the apparition of the woman he alone could see, he never was aware of the train that came thundering down upon him. It struck at the same time that the wraith woman faded and vanished.

In limbo, Shari had her first feeling of release. She had not lifted a finger against Bert. His own guilty conscience had brought him to justice. Shari was blameless.

A shaft of light from above enveloped her. Smiling serenely, Shari floated up, ascending into the Higher Level.

VOICES OF CHILDREN

"I don't believe in love at first sight." She was a small, slim girl with blue eyes and shoulder length, blonde hair. It was the first session of college evening classes. She had hurried into the Psychology 103 classroom fifteen minutes early and there were already about a dozen students seated about. She chose a third-row seat on the middle aisle, took her spiral-bound, hardcover notebook and a pen out of a black portfolio which she zipped closed, then stashed on the wooden slats under her chair.

Her gaze went to the open door, watching as others came into the room. She didn't expect to see any familiar face because this was her first term and she had come from out of town. Most of those who entered were singles, but two girls came in, chatting amiably, stopping for a brief moment to check the door number, say, "This is it," and head for the back row where they could continue talking.

He entered, a moment behind them and checked the room number. Stepping over the threshold, he stopped and glanced about. A slight young man, wearing poplin gray shorts and matching sweatshirt with the college logo, he had knotted the sleeves of a sweater about his shoulders. He had dark wavy hair and his dark eyes swept the room and met her gaze.

She felt that she could never take her eyes from his. A feeling of belonging enveloped her—so strong, so intense that she knew she had fallen instantly and completely in love with him. Through her mind flashed the romantic stories she had read of bells ringing, of lights flashing, of stars falling to earth. None of those were actually happening, yet she experienced the same wild, inexplicable thrill.

He came over instantly, took the vacant seat beside her, put his portfolio on the desk of the chair and reached out his right hand to take her left hand in his.

"My name is Ir," he introduced in a low tone.

"Ir? Is that short for Irwin?"

He cocked his head to one side, regarding her, "Why, yes, I suppose. And yours?" She told him, just as the instructor entered and placed his briefcase on the desk. He turned to the blackboard, wrote his name with chalk and underneath wrote the class and room number. "Check your student cards," he advised, "If this information is not on the left hand corner, you are in the wrong place. Leave now and find your correct class. I will call your name. Bring up your card."

Two men left the room. The others prepared their I.D.s for collection. When her name was called, she brought the instructor hers.

"Ir Winn," the teacher called. He placed his card on the pile and resumed his seat.

The introduction and list of textbooks needed for the course and a preliminary overview of the term's work took the next forty-minutes.

"There is a ten minute break here," the teacher advised. "I am available for anything you wish to discuss."

As some pupils came to the desk, Ir asked, "Are you ready to leave now?"

She nodded. It seemed pointless to stay when she knew that her life was about to take a totally different turn from all that she had planned before tonight.

Everything seemed so natural. They left the classroom. She led the way to the student parking lot, unlocked the doors of her Toyota and slid behind the wheel, as he slid into the passenger side.

"Do you live in the dorm?" He asked.

She shook her head. "I have a one-bedroom with kitchen about a block from here. I have no roommate."

"Till now." he smiled.

In her tiny kitchenette she prepared two tuna sandwiches and milk for their supper. As they ate, she told him about herself. "Daddy died when I was six and mom raised me alone. We had no relatives. Last year mom died and I decided to sell our house and use the money to come east and register in college for elementary education. I love kids and want to be a teacher."

"I'm glad you love kids."

"It was my dream to get married. Being an only child I wanted to have lots of children."

He smiled, put the remnants of his sandwich on the plate and reached for her hand. "That's why I'm here. Didn't you guess as soon as we saw each other that we were meant for each other?"

There should have been questions she needed to ask. There were answers she should know. It did not seem important. Everything appeared to be happening as if planned. She rose, leading the way to the bedroom.

Later, he murmured close to her ear. "You are with child now."

Drowsy with contentment, she said, "And will it be a girl or a boy?" She meant it to be flippant since he seemed so positive, not only of the pregnancy, but the sex of the child, but he answered, quite seriously and without hesitation: "A girl, of course. That's the whole purpose."

"Purpose?" She shook off the pleasant lethargy, "I don't understand."

"I should have told you everything when we were talking at the table, but you seemed so ready, I put it off."

She stared at him not knowing what on earth he was talking about. "Put off telling me what?"

"Who I am and why I am here."

"To meet me, of course."

"Definitely. That was my mission. I was sent to find you. I found you and loved you."

"Mission? Loved me? This was intended?"

"You might say it was meant to be."

"By whom?"

"By me. And by my people."

"What people?"

He sat up and drew her up, turning her face so they could look right into each other's eyes. Mirrored in his, was his love for her. And her eyes reflected the same.

"You guessed from the moment we met that I was not of your world. And you knew it didn't matter. But in all honesty I need to tell you that I was sent, just for this purpose, to find you, to love you and to give you our daughter."

"Daughter?"

"She will be born next month. Her name is Em."

"Emily … what a nice name. But it takes nine months.…"

"Not the children of our seed. I was sent from another galaxy because our women have contracted a virus and cannot be saved. We need other women to bear female babies to repopulate our world."

"But aren't your men affected?"

"Our men are not susceptible to the virus, neither are alien women. We impregnate females not of our world. These don't carry the virus, so we are able to repopulate our planet. I did not mean to hide this from you, or make love to you under false pretenses. It is not the mission alone that sent me in search of you, I always knew that you were somewhere in the universe, waiting for me, as I was waiting for you. Can you forgive my deception?"

She knew it was no deception. She had always known he would be coming. She had dreams about it as far back as she could recall. She did not know when he would come, or from where, or how he would look. But he was here and she was complete. That was all that mattered.

"If the child will be born soon, we won't be able to stay here—or stay in one place." She had always been practical. But he was reassuring.

"I've made all the arrangements." He took the portfolio from beside the bed where he had put it when they undressed. Opening it, he unzipped one compartment. There were large bills, stacked and bound. Many stacks. "Money is no object. And neither is a place to live. I'll go out tomorrow and buy an RV in which we can live and travel and have the baby without rousing any suspicion."

"Answer a question for me."

"Anything."

"How can I bear a baby in a month?"

"Because I am not from Earth. Our time span works differently. Ask how old I am."

She did. Somehow his answer did not surprise or shock her.

"I am five years old. We mature faster, but once we have reached maturity, as I have, we stabilize and live much longer than your Earth years. Are there any other questions?"

She found it a little hard to ask, "Do you need to find another female to impregnate now?"

He smiled. "No. We are monogamous. Like many of your Earth birds and animals, we find one mate and remain faithful. Any other questions?"

"No." She was satisfied. They were going to be together and soon the first of their daughters would be born. She came back into his embrace. "There was a poet named William Blake," she told him. "He wrote:

> When the voices of children are heard on the green
> And laughing is heard on the hill,
> My heart is at rest within my breast,
> And everything else is still."

They stayed in her apartment for a week. Then he went out to purchase an RV while she gave notice to the superintendent of her building that she was leaving town. She gave him an envelope for the entire rent owed, plus a month's security which she considered forfeit due to her hasty termination of the contract.

She packed the few possessions she owned and finished just as Ir returned to help carry the suitcases down and stash them while she turned in her apartment keys. Outside, she found him waiting at the wheel of the new motor-home which would be their house from now on.

They had to be on the move. Otherwise suspicion would surely be roused due to the fast-changing condition of her body. Her pregnancy became more apparent each day, showing changes so rapidly that only moving amongst strangers could conceal the abnormality.

At the end of the month she went into labor. Ir skillfully delivered the baby girl, after a short painless delivery. Even the child revealed no wrinkling or mucous-like afterbirth. He washed the infant with soothing ointments that left her smooth and sweet smelling and when he put her in her mother's arms, the milk began to flow in her breasts and the baby began to feed at once.

Motherhood! She could not get over the wonder of the experience! Em was a most perfectly formed infant and each day she matured, developing into a child. Although the mother in her vaguely yearned to have a longer period of infancy, she was fascinated by the daily changes that took place.

Within two weeks, Em had her baby teeth and delighted in gnawing on a lamb chop bone. There had not been any teething problems accompanied by fretful restlessness. She no longer required breast feeding and was able to eat like a toddler. She had no difficulty sitting, after just a few days of pulling herself up on the bars of the crib. After that it was an easy step to hauling herself upright, clinging to the crib bar. She swayed a bit at first, but soon was standing as sturdy as any toddler.

By the time she was a month old, she was out of the creeper stage and walking about the interior of the motor home. It was not necessary to warn her of dangers of tripping on electric cords, or touching the stove when it was lit. She appeared to have an innate sense of safety and managed to avoid problems that other human babies might encounter.

At two months she was walking, talking and looked like a toddler. At three months she was reading and looked like a preschooler.

Ir said, "Now you understand why it was important for us to live in a motor home. We could never have stayed where earth people could see the rapid changes in Em. We would have been reported. Government agents would have investigated. We would have been locked in laboratories for endless testing and observation...."

"Has that happened before?" He shrugged. "It will not happen. It is just a possibility, so we must be ever vigilant. We will remain on Earth a little longer. Em will develop quickly."

"I love Em. I should be sad that she has such a short babyhood for me to enjoy. Why do I feel a sense of gladness?"

"Because your next little girl can be conceived when you desire."

She reached out to take his hand. "Ir, where do I fit in after that?"

He studied her. "Where would you like to fit?"

"I—I know what I would like. I don't know if I can—or if it will be allowed...."

Dozens of difficulties seemed to pop into her mind. He watched her quietly. She realized he was expecting her to come to some decision, without his prompting. "I would like to go with you—to return to your world—but I don't know if that would be allowed, or if I could physically make the changeover."

He laughed out loud, his voice revealing a relief as though he had feared she would never consent to such a choice. "Of course, you could come with us. That is the thing we most wanted, but feared you would not consider. Oh, my dear love, don't you remember me telling you I was monogamous—that meant I could have no life without you from now on."

Relief and happiness flooded her so fully that she could not stop the tears from flowing. It had lain in her heart since she had first seen him—the fear that he would need to go away and not be able to take her.

The only thing she could think of saying while exhilaration filled her was, "When can we start another baby girl?"

He laughed with delight. "Now, if you wish."

The time flew after that. When Em reached six months, her baby sister, Tee, was born.

The day that was scheduled for the meeting with the spaceship was approaching.

Ir drove the motor home to the designated spot—an isolated hilltop far from human habitation. Their vehicle would not be able to make it through the roadless way, so they stopped at the last gas station where Ir told the owner they needed money and would sell the motor home to him for one-fourth of its value.

Delighted with his bargain, the man gave him the cash and watched the couple and their two children walk off into the sparse scrub and the thin trees of the desolate area where, Ir had said, other parents would be meeting them.

It was a six-mile hike along sandy dunes and skeletal woods. Uphill going might have been difficult had it not been for their youth and the goal of their destination.

The spaceship appeared to be a glowing cloud, gaseous and pulsing with a life of its own. On the crest of the hill, it waited, while—from all directions—came the passengers who would be on it when it left Earth and went out into the galaxy.

There were no apertures. They came to it and it enveloped them.

Ir led the way, holding Tee by the hand. Em, with the impatience of a child, shook free of her mother's hand and dashed after them. Her mother had to turn around, knowing this would be her last sight of the planet on which she had been born.

She heard Ir call to her. "Hurry, we're the last to board. Hurry. We're going home. *Eve! Eve!*"

MIRROR, MIRROR, ON THE WALL

As she dropped the gun and staggered backwards, David Wentworth, her psychiatrist, observed how similar her acting-out was at every session, since she had begun coming to him weekly, for the past two months. She always began with her dream of shooting her older sister, Eloise.

He suspected she suffered from a dual personality disorder.

"It wasn't fair of Daddy to leave everything to Elly!"

Mandy's brown hair was cut in a pageboy style; her brown eyes had never—in all the times he had seen her—relaxed into a happy mood. He concluded she could never solve her problems while battling her sister's personality, seeking her own identity.

The reading of the will was the primary reason Mandy had sought a psychiatrist. Vehement about daddy's will, she did admit, in all honesty, that Eloise unselfishly shared everything with her.

"Elly promised I'd continue to live in the house with her. Even when she married Kenneth three years ago; even when Ken was killed in an automobile accident a year ago; and even when her baby girl Jessica was born six months ago."

"Then you're lucky."

"I'd be luckier inheriting everything! You really need to see for yourself how impossible it is to compete against her. Everyone loves Elly. Mama loved her right up to the moment she died giving birth to me. I'm twenty years old and haven't had a life of my own. Being in the shadow of a beautiful sister doesn't get me much attention. If it had been me, in Elly's place, I'd have hated the little sister who caused Mama's death. But Elly isn't like that. She tries to take care of me. But I'm sure she resents me."

"Maybe she really cares for you."

"Why not decide for yourself? Come to the house. Meet Elly. You'll be deceived by her beauty and sweetness. Everyone is. If she weren't mourning for Ken, she'd have boyfriends all the time. I thought Ken's death would end that, but I was wrong!"

David caught a strange look in her eyes. Vengeful? It was so fleeting, so quickly veiled, that he thought he was mistaken. But that momentary impression left him uneasy, suspecting that Mandy had somehow caused Kenneth's death....

Curious, David drove to the house where Mandy lived. He parked, went up to the door, rang the bell and waited, hearing the light clicking of high heels, approaching.

The door was opened by a stunning girl.

"Dr. Wentworth," she held out her slim hands. "I'm Eloise, Mandy's sister. Please come in." She led the way into a large living room with plump couches and easy chairs. He took a seat on the sofa, as she sat opposite, on the love seat.

"Mandy said you were beautiful," he smiled in approval of her slim figure in lilac pantsuit, which complemented her amazing violet eyes. Her red-gold hair was shoulder length and her skin, devoid of make-up was honeyed from the sun. Small wonder that Mandy was jealous, he thought.

Eloise explained, "I've loved Mandy since birth; I never meant to make her feel unwanted. Aunt Grace is the only one with no patience for Mandy."

"Aunt Grace?" It was a new name to the doctor.

"Aunt Grace is daddy's unmarried sister. She lives with us. When the baby was born, she took over Jesse's care. She's invaluable—especially to me—because I teach English at Brentwood College. You can see it from the window."

He went over and saw the spire of the college library building up on a high slope of hill, perhaps a mile into town.

A tall, gray-haired, stylishly dressed woman entered the room. "Aunt Grace," Eloise introduced, "This is Dr. David Wentworth." The woman had sharp eyes, looking like a faded edition of Eloise's high coloring. She said, "I thought the doctor might like to see Jesse."

She led them upstairs to a room with mother-goose wallpaper and white nursery furniture. Motioning the doctor to the crib, Aunt Grace smiled lovingly at the baby whose feet kicked the air energetically. The doctor looked at the cooing child.

Jessica had her mother's lilac eyes. Her fine hair was the same red-gold as Eloise's. The doorbell rang. "I'll get it," Eloise said and headed downstairs.

As soon as she left Aunt Grace said, "Come downstairs. I want to show you something in the garden."

"But you have company."

She grimaced. "It's only *him*! Cullen White! That rotten boy Mandy insists on calling a friend. He was expelled from Brentwood College in his freshman year. They found blasting caps, wires and dynamite in his room. He was experimenting with bomb making. Now he's threatened the college for expelling him. A bad seed!"

Aunt Grace drew David downstairs. She opened a door that led into the back garden. A path led between flowers and shrubs. At the far end was a foot high fence, enclosing a grassy plot containing two graves. The headstone on a full sized grave read: "Dorothy Carter, beloved wife and mother, died in childbirth at the age of thirty-two."

A smaller marker on a child-size grave read: "Mandy Carter: Died at birth."

The horror of what the tombstone implied struck David with shocking force. In a hoarse, unbelieving whisper he told Aunt Grace, "I suspected dual personality. But I never suspected...."

Aunt Grace supplied: "Possession ...?"

Spoken aloud, the word took on an aspect of superstition born in the dark ignorance of antiquity. Despite training in modern medicine, David's skin crawled. He had offered guidance to a girl who was not even alive!

"Mandy wouldn't accept death, so she lived vicariously—through Eloise."

"Didn't their father know?"

"He knew. He tried psychiatrists. Doctors. Priests. Exorcists. They kept Mandy weak for a long time. She couldn't spoil Eloise's life completely. But Eloise was too kind, too guilt-ridden that she lived and Mandy did not. Eloise should have fought harder. I told her. The doctors told her. But she wanted to share with Mandy. Now Mandy's getting older, learning how to take over, more and more. God help us if she succeeds!" Suddenly, she froze. They heard the motor of a car, starting up.

Grace's face turned ashen white. "They're leaving!" Wildly she turned to him. "I didn't expect it so soon!" He was completely at a loss. The fear in her face was real, her urgency so immediate, that he felt as though a door was being opened, spewing out wild, unmentionable things. He was not wrong!

Feeling a panic that he could not explain, he allowed her to draw him along as she hastened out of the garden.

The two who had been in the living room were no longer there. The front door was open!

Aunt Grace went out and stood on the top step, the doctor beside her. He could see she was in great fear of something she expected to happen.

"It's Mandy's doing!" she cried, trembling with frightened agitation. "She's got that weasel Cullen to help her!"

"Help her do what?"

"Why, kill Eloise, of course!"

"But she wouldn't do that! She knows killing Eloise is fatal to herself. She needs Eloise's body!"

As though to give the lie to his words, there occurred such a tremendous explosion that even as they looked across where the college stood, they could feel the tremors and see the flames and hear the bombardment that tore apart buildings, streets, stores. Cars, like toys, flew up in the air and smashed down. The mighty roar of devastation drowned out the screams of the injured and the dying....

Despairingly, Aunt Grace cried, "Mandy's killed Eloise!"

Upstairs, the baby began to cry.

Aunt Grace's routines as caretaker were strong. She had to fight the sickness and the horrified awareness inside her. The baby needed her.

As she hurried up the stairs, David followed. Only a moment or two behind, he entered the room.

He saw her bend to lift the child. He saw her stop, grow rigid! He heard her give a scream, so filled with fear, with disbelief, with unutterable terror, that it froze his blood.

He rushed forward. He looked down at the baby. Unspeakable alarm and dread overpowered him. The baby's lilac eyes were losing luster. Darkening—like a cloud over the sun—they changed. They became brown.

The fine red-gold hair altered. It turned dark—a dull-toned brown. The smiling, dimpled features took on a different expression. Sullen, lips drawn down at the corners, the child's face assumed a disgruntled look.

"Oh, God help us!" Aunt Grace moaned, covering her eyes with shaking hands. "Mandy has possession of Jessica now! Help us! Help us, God! Mandy is alive again!"

ABRACADABRA

"Look! I just want you to listen to my story. I've got to tell someone and you're alone at this back table of the bar. Your chin's inside your turtleneck and your knitted cap's pulled over your face so no one should notice you sleeping over your beer. Okay. I'd just as soon you don't hear my horror story. You'd have nightmares, too.

It began one evening after work. Ma had supper ready, as always. Her heart condition didn't stop her from keeping our tenement apartment orderly. Dad died five years ago. Ma and I were all we had. Maybe it wasn't right for a thirty year old to live with his mother, but I was shy with ladies and didn't make friends easily. Our routines were suitable.

Who would expect life to change just by taking out the garbage? But that's what happened. I took our plastic bag into the alley. As I raised the hopper lid, a cat jumped off the top and hit the ground. There was something white and fluttering in its mouth. A bird, I thought with pity, as I snatched the cat up by its scruff. As soon as he squalled in protest, I caught the fluttering thing out of his jaws, then shooed the cat away. I looked at what I'd rescued.

Astonished, I almost dropped it. It was no bird. It was a wiggling, diminutive female, half the size of my palm. Dressed in a gossamer shift that floated ankle-length to her bare feet, she had tiny wings that sprouted through slits in the shoulders of the green-sleeved frock. An angel, I thought. I've caught an angel!

"I'm Titania," she introduced, "and you're holding me too tightly, Frank Morrow!"

She knew my name! I almost released her in surprise, but caution stopped me. I remembered—captured sprites grant wishes for freedom. "For three wishes, I'll release you."

She made a face. "That tiresome game! There are rules and a contract. I give wishes, you give me something. What's your first wish?"

Totally unprepared, my mind raced. "I always wanted to be a millionaire."

"Done! Now let go!"

"Wait! Is there a time period before something happens?"

"Depends on the wish. Nothing begins until we say the password. Choose a word!"

A childish memory stirred. "If you say Abracadabra, I become a millionaire?"

"That starts the process. Sometimes it's instantaneous. Sometimes it takes days, even weeks. Meantime, you give me a small payment." I looked at my school ring, but she said, "No, I'll take something from your personality."

For a million dollars, she could have my eyeteeth. I released her. "Abracadabra!" she said and disappeared.

"Ma," I shouted, running into the house, "Guess what happened!"

Ma, in front of the TV set, fell sideways when I touched her. Her heart had stopped; she was dead. The next days bustled. Funeral arrangements, bank accounts, Social Security, phone calls. Despite taking time off, it was hectic.

Finally, I was home alone. The doorbell rang. The man at the door said he represented an insurance company. Seated opposite me, he said my mother left a policy. I was sole beneficiary of one million dollars! In my mind I heard, "Abracadabra!" I had become a millionaire!

I gave up my job. An auctioneer sold everything in the apartment. I signed for a condo near Central Park and rented furniture while seeking a decorator. I called, "Titania!" She instantly appeared. "For my second wish I want a beautiful girl to love me!"

"Abracadabra," she said and disappeared.

I took the telephone directory. Under *Interior Decorators*, one ad caught my attention: *A. Starr, specializing in custom treatments. Make your dream house come true. Wish upon A. STARR.* The ad seemed magically meant for me. I dialed the number. A sweet voice announced, "This is Amanda Starr."

When she arrived, I knew she was *the* girl! A stunning brunette, with hair pulled back into a chignon, She reminded me of a dark-haired Evita.

Amanda was as professional as she was beautiful. At twenty-five she owned a successful business. In less than a month she had draperies, wall coverings and carpeting, exactly to my specifications. She mirrored the closets, tables and doors to achieve spaciousness. A beveled cheval mirror was placed in the entrance hall for a final inspection before going out.

With the apartment completed, we got married. Amanda continued working. I had retired. I found time dragging; I grew irritable if she was delayed by clients.

One day I slapped her. With the welt of my hand on her cheek, I was amazed to feel no regret, except for a strong concern not to mar her beauty. The next time I struck her it was with an open-handed body blow. After that, it was with a closed fist—but never to her face.

I felt no remorse about abusing Amanda. I did not fear her leaving or reporting me. Power offered reassurance. Nevertheless I was perplexed. Cruelty was out of my character, I had been a loving son. Yet, when Ma died, I didn't cry. Now, I even looked forward to Amanda's punishments.

When she stepped inside the door, I was waiting.

At my expression, she began whimpering, "Darling, please, I've done nothing." I moved, fists clenched. Sobbing, she turned to run. I shoved her in the back with all my might, sending her, head first, into the tailor's mirror. Both fell crashing!

The mirror fragments, large and jagged, small and pulverized, littered the floor beneath her. Blood spurted, mixed with the murderous slivers.

I was thunderstruck. I'd never planned this. Gingerly stepping to her side, I bent—turned her face-up. Glass had penetrated her skin. Her face was lacerated beyond imagining.

In the hospital I reported it as an accident. When Amanda was fitfully conscious, she murmured, "I fell against the mirror...." Her beauty was gone. The gashes had gone to the bone. Plastic surgery couldn't repair the damage. I went home. Servants had repaired everything. No sliver or bloodstain remained where Amanda had fallen.

For days I stayed in, my mind churning with anger. I took no blame for Amanda's lost beauty. I didn't visit, call, or send flowers, remaining sunk in self-pity at my loss. I stayed closeted in my apartment, not answering the doorbell or telephone. Eventually the shock wore off. My mind began to function again. I still had a third wish!

"Titania!" I summoned. She appeared. Without preamble I said, "I want my wife's beauty restored!"

"It will take time...."

"Get it done! And answer this truthfully—what did you take from me to seal our contract?"

"Your conscience," she said. And vanished.

I remained at home; the days passed. One day, in the far reaches of my mind, I heard the signal. "Abracadabra!" Out of the house I ran and took a cab to the hospital. Up to Amanda's room I raced. The bed was freshly made. The room was empty. "Nurse! Where's my wife, Amanda Morrow."

With sympathy she said, "She died yesterday. We tried to reach you...."

"Where is she?"

The nurse handed me a card. "At this funeral parlor."

I rushed to hail a cab and get to the address listed. I identified myself to the director. He led me to a room. There was a coffin on a raised dais. "The hospital said you wanted the best for your wife." In the coffin of polished wood and gleaming brass, Amanda lay amongst lace and satin. The embalmer had done a masterful job of reconstructive makeup. Amanda's beauty was fully restored. Far off in my mind, I heard, "*Abracadabra!*"

I rushed home and summoned Titania. "You tricked me! Everything you did for me was evil! What kind of an angel are you?"

"I never said I was an angel! You assumed that! I'm an imp—from hell. And now my lord will finalize the contract." She was gone.

So here I am in this murky seaman's bar, wondering what happens next.

"I can tell you that," said my table-companion.

I looked up, startled. The features opposite were revealed—slanted green eyes in a crimson face, with horns curving through the knit seaman's cap. Horror filled me. Across the table, a hand reached and caught my wrist in a talon claw.

"The contract has been satisfactorily fulfilled," Satan said, "You're mine now."

And—before we both vanished from that place—he smiled and whispered roguishly,
"Abracadabra!"

ABUSER

The child's screams pierced the evening air from the open first floor window. Melanie was just driving around the corner toward her parking place. Her radio was on and she did not hear her daughter's cries. Pulling to a stop, she went to the trunk for her two shopping bags. Key in hand, she opened the building door. Kept locked for security reasons, only tenants had access.

Once inside, a long flight of steps faced her, dimly lit by a bulb of low wattage. The landlord economized wherever possible. Melanie tended to excuse him. It was only a four-tenant building and Mr. Miles himself occupied the ground floor railroad flat, so his income was solely from his three tenants and Melanie was grateful that her monthly rent was only $450, which was pretty nominal for a two-bedroom with a spacious living room and a large eat-in kitchen.

It was made more pleasant by the grassy backyard, which Mr. Miles had fenced in himself. He boasted of being handy with tools. He had erected a storage and tool shed just to the right of the door, leading into the yard. He did not lock the shed. Tenants were permitted to store lounge chairs, which they could set up on the grass and sun themselves in the yard. They were reminded to "pick up after themselves." And they did—not wanting to lose the privilege of enjoying a bit of country living on this city street of brownstones and tenements.

Melanie was halfway upstairs when she froze. Screams, punctuated by, "Don't! Don't!" blasted from her apartment. Icy chills went through her. She recognized the cries of her eight-year old daughter Jaimysue.

Prayerfully, Melanie raced up, her trembling fingers searching for the right key on the ring. Dropping her packages on the worn carpeting, she inserted the key, twisting it and the knob at the same time. Flinging the door open, she rushed into the living room. The appalling scene before her eyes, immobilized her!

At the far end, in front of the long window, was the chintz-covered couch. She could see Jaimysue lying on it, elbow over eyes, clothes disheveled. A tall man hunched over her.

"Stuart!" Melanie shouted, "Stop it! Stop! Stop!"

The man whirled. His expression was distraught. "Mel, thank god, you're here!" he cried. Melanie flew across the room, shoving the man aside. "Jaimysue! Baby, are you all right?" Her daughter, on her back on the couch, had been wearing a striped white and pink polo with matching striped shorts. The shirt was jaggedly cut from the neck down and her sunburnt flesh showed bare. Whirling, Melanie beheld Stuart, holding large shears in hand. Seeing the direction of her horror-filled gaze, he looked down and appeared stupefied at the sight of the shears, dropping them as though they were hot.

"Are you crazy?" Melanie screamed at him. "Why did you cut Jaimysue's shirt?" He looked at her, stunned. "Cut?" he asked. "Cut?" He shook his head. "No, Mel, I didn't...."

Jaimysue sobbed, "Mommy, he hurt me!"

Melanie dropped to her knees on the floor. Gathering the crying child in a comforting embrace, she rocked and soothed her. "It's all right. Mommy's here! You're safe! No one is going to hurt you!"

"Stuart will! He slapped me!"

The excuse from the big man sounded inane, unsure, "I only shook her ... trying to stop her hysterics...."

"You slapped me!" the child accused.

"Because you were screaming...."

Melanie tried to get to the bottom of the matter. "Why?" she asked the man, "Why was she screaming? What were you doing to her?" Melanie's own heart plunged, as she felt compelled to ask the question. She and Stuart had been living together for six months and she could not imagine an incident between him and her daughter. They had always seemed so compatible. He seemed so kind, caring and loving. What on earth had triggered this unbelievable incident?

Suddenly Stuart appeared to realize how the scene must have appeared and tried to explain, "Honestly, Mel, I haven't a clue. I was on the bedroom phone when I thought I heard Jaimysue make strange noises...." He stopped, groping for the right words.

"I thought she was choking or something. I hung up the phone. When I came into the living room Jaimysue's back was toward me. I asked her what was wrong. She turned around. She was cutting her polo shirt. I rushed to grab the scissors from her. She began to scream. I tried to talk to her, but she just kept yelling and yelling. I didn't know how to make her stop. I began to shake her. She collapsed on the couch, shouting, "Don't! Don't!" I thought she was hysterical and slapped her to bring her out of it. Then, thank god, you came in."

"Mommy! Mommy!" the little girl sobbed. "He cut my blouse! He slapped me!" She flung herself into her mother's embrace. Putting her lips close to her ear, she whispered, "Mommy, he touched me! Stuart touched me!"

Shocked beyond reason, Melanie could only think to hug her daughter closer, rock her and repeat over and over, "It's all right, baby! Everything's all right now. Mommy's here! No one will hurt you!"

Stuart looked at the two, his gaze unbelieving. "What do you mean, 'No one will hurt you'? No one hurt her before. Mel, you can't seriously believe I hurt her!" He fell silent, unable to find words to refute what was being implied. He was a tall man, nearly six foot, Yet, he suddenly sagged into the easy chair, his face growing pale He put his hand against his mouth. The stress had made his lips tremble.

"Mel," he whispered, "I didn't do what you're thinking…."

"You did! You did!" Jaimysue repeated. "You shook me! You slapped me!"

Melanie looked over her daughter's head. "Stuart," she said with quiet steeliness, "I don't think you should stay here tonight."

He rose. He said, heavily, "I'll go to a motel." After he left, Jaimysue had her bath and her supper. It was nice having mommy all to herself. "Can I sleep with you tonight?" she asked. "Of course, baby."

It was so good being in the bed with mommy and being cuddled again. Only it didn't last long. It took a few weeks, but Stuart kept phoning and sending flowers and finally Melanie accepted his story that Jaimysue had merely been hysterical and that he had never made any overt moves against her.

All was well for two months. Then, once again Melanie was returning home. Like deja vu she heard her daughter pleading and screaming. And this time when she burst into the apartment her child and her boyfriend were in the bedroom. Jaimysue's dress was up, her panties on the floor and Stuart was saying through clenched teeth, "Be still! Be quiet!"

She was flailing the air and he was catching her arms, holding them and demanding: "Stop fighting! Lie still!" Melanie flew at him. Like a tiger she raked his back, pulling him away from the child.

He turned to face her. She yelled, "You MONSTER! What a fool I was to let you come back. But this time I won't let you get away with your attack!"

She reached for the telephone. Pressed the "0" and when the operator answered, Melanie said, "Get me the police!"

He was protesting when they handcuffed him and led him away, with Melanie cuddling her daughter, insisting she would be at the station in the morning to file charges.

She didn't need to do so. In the morning a policeman was at her door. Stuart had hanged himself in his jail cell during the night.

Melanie's face turned white. The young officer caught her, just as her knees gave way. Gently, he set her in the easy chair. Into the kitchen he went and returned with some cold water. He held the glass while she sipped.

"Is there anyone who can be with you?" he inquired. She shook her head.

He told her, "Don't worry. I'll stay to make sure you're all right."

Standing behind the door, watching, Jaimysue saw the way things were going. Now she realized what the problem was. Her mother was just too pretty. It wouldn't matter how many men Jaimysue would get rid of; there would always be others. She could see how it was going again. This policeman would be mommy's next boyfriend. Jaimysue had to give this even more thought than she had done in the past.

Mommy was the problem!

Gnawing at her finger nails, Jaimysue thought and thought. She knew that in the storage shed the landlord kept tools and paints and all manner of cleanser and electrical materials. He had told Melanie he would keep the caustic bottles on the uppermost shelf.

"Can't have your young one reach it. If it spilled on her, it would scar her for life."

It was true it was high on the shelf, but there was also a five-foot ladder Jaimysue could climb and take the bottle to pour one night on mommy's face.

Jaimysue knew the label well. An easy name to read and there was a skull and crossbones label of warning. "L-Y-E."

After that, no one else would get into bed with mommy and Jaimysue would have mommy all to herself again.

BETH'S STORY

Just because I am ten years old, don't think my problems aren't as important to me as grown-ups' problems are to them. It isn't easy living with "NO" most of your life. My folks say I don't appreciate the things I've got. I know that there are poor children who don't have enough to eat, but how does it help them if I have to eat stuff I hate just because it's good for me? Or how does it help poor children who have no real beds to sleep in that I have a nice clean bed of my own, but have to get in it and go to sleep by eight?

We live in a beautiful ranch house in Upland, California. Most folks never heard of Upland, so when they ask where I live in California, I say Los Angeles. Everyone's heard of that and then they understand, so I don't have to go through explanations about where I live. We have a large backyard, with a free-form pool. It can be heated, too, but when we ask dad, he says, "Not now." He's always too busy, so my twelve-year-old sister Dana and I swim in it and finally get used to the cool water.

In our family we are four—mom and dad and Dana and me. Dana is older, but has cerebral palsy and lupus and because of the palsy, she is a slow learner and goes to special classes in school. My mom has lupus, too and has to go to the hospital for check-ups all the time. I hate when that happens.

I get so angry, that I have to blame someone, so I blame my mom. I blame her for being sick and I blame my mom because my sister is sick. Mom says that's a bad attitude to have, but what else can I do? I can't blame God. That's a sin. Besides, I wouldn't want God to be angry with me. I'd rather have God on my side all the time, so that lets Him out of being blamed.

Sometimes I yell at my dad and I cry and tell him he should see things my way and do things I want to do. If I keep that up, he finally gets real mad. That's like getting angry at God. You can't win.

So here I am, all full of mad, mad feelings. When anyone tells me I'm wrong about something, I look at them as if they are crazy. I can't think of myself as being wrong. I think I'm a very nice girl and pretty smart and easy to get along with. And when others don't see me like that, I think they are crazy and it makes me angry.

Dad says I have the bad habit of taking credit for everything good that happens, but won't admit to anything bad that happens. He says I always yell, "It wasn't my fault," even if it is. He reminds me of the time our grandma came and took me shopping in the mall. She gave me $10 and I picked out a purse I liked. Then I picked out another one for Dana and she paid for that, too.

When I came home I told everyone I had bought it and when dad said, "Where did you get the money?" I said Grandma gave the money to me. "Then *she* bought the bags," he said. "You just picked them out." Well, he was right, but I wouldn't admit it and kept saying, "I gave the saleslady the money and I picked out the bags, so I bought them!" And I wouldn't thank Grandma.

I think how nice it would be if my sister were a regular twelve-year-old without all those sicknesses. Wouldn't it have made my life better, to have a sister who goes to regular classes and does things that normal girls do?

Friends who have teen brothers or sisters don't think it's so hot to have them. Their brothers or sisters think they are pests and try to get rid of them all the time. It's true that Dana and I fight a lot, but we also miss each other when she goes to camp and I stay home or go somewhere else. Even if we argue, we also do a lot of talking together and we do play together. It's better with her than without her.

If I were to put myself in Dana's place I know that I would be happy that I was born into our family. Mom and dad do everything they can to help her overcome her handicaps. Mom was the Girl Scout leader until she got too sick to go on. Now dad shares the leadership with one of the other Scouts' mother.

My sister won a gold medal in the Olympics for special children. She could never have been a winner without my mom's encouragement and help. I think Dana knows that and I know that I should remember things like that, but I get too busy being furious and, instead of saying nice things, I start to say, "Well, why didn't you do this and why didn't you do that?" and "If you had done it my way it would have been better. It's your fault, your fault."

Why do I blame my mom just because not everything is perfect in our lives? I wish I knew. I wish I knew why I say things to hurt her, when I know how bad it makes me feel, when anyone says mean things that hurt me. I don't mean hurt like a smack in the face; I mean hurt feelings.

Hurt feelings can get you down and leave you sad for a long time, maybe even days, or a week at a stretch. You find yourself thinking about getting even with whoever hurt your feelings. But you never think that moms don't get even when children hurt *their* feelings.

I have to remind myself that mom did not want to be sick. She suffers and she cries. Nobody wants that to happen to themselves. And no one wants their child to suffer. My mom is a good mom and I love her. I know she loves me.

Someone told me that grown-ups get just as scared as we kids. I don't really understand that and I find it hard to believe. It seems to me that grown-ups can do what they want and go where they want. They don't have to get permission from anybody. So, if they get scared, they can go away on vacation. They can find someplace to go to forget the scary things. But if it's true that grown-ups can't just escape from the things that frighten them, then I must stop blaming you, mom, for things that you can't change.

I say I love you, but I know that if I really love you, I should try to keep you from being frightened at what the doctors say about your condition.

I should try to be a good child, a good daughter and a good friend. I would talk to you nicely, not crying and angry like a child, but quiet and comforting— like a friend—like a real good, best friend. I would tell you everything will be okay and the doctors will make you well soon. I know this won't be easy for me to do, because I'm not really good. I am too angry all the time.

Don't think I don't know I should be honest enough—and kind enough—to admit my family does wonderful things for me and to realize that they do those things—not because they would be put in jail if they didn't—but because they want to do the best they can. And I should, too. I shouldn't hide the good side and only let the mean side come out.

My dad always says, "Your trouble is that you want what you want when you want it!"

I'm not really sure I understand. But, when I think about it, it does sound just like me. What do you think?

COMPUTERS—A WORLD I NEVER MADE

Progress tends to drag us forward, despite our most determined intentions to remain detached.

I am a four-foot-eleven woman; there aren't many things shorter than I. But our computer is. So why am I intimidated by this midget monster?

For years we had a computer in our home. My husband and children are experts. I have done my duty—dusting it, cleaning the glass and case and giving it as much attention as I would one of our closets, but less attention than if it were a television. We have a mutual understanding. You stay in your place and I'll stay in mine.

The new vocabulary that develops all around me falls on sterile ears. After all, what do I have to do with Megabytes? Gigabytes? Databases? CD-ROMs?

A mouse, to me, has always meant a rodent—one I would never consider touching, dead or alive. Yet, here I am, holding a mouse, clicking a mouse and using it to open new horizons on the monitor—*the monitor?* That used to be a child assigned to assist me in my classroom. Now it turns out to be the screen of my computer—and I must follow its rules, because if I don't, an error can result in terrible consequences—the most horrifying being the anguished cries of my husband, "What did you do to this computer? I can't bring up my income tax records? Did you put them in the trash?"

With guilt and contrition, I assure, "I'll look right away," and start scrounging in the wastepaper basket.

"No! No! Not that—the computer trash!"

Computer trash, like the mouse, isn't the same as the trash we have known from childhood, which goes out into a garbage can and gets collected by garbage men. The computer trash, I discover, has the science-fiction ability to disintegrate matter—maybe never to return! Seeing my husband's expression I begin to wonder if I should apply for the Witness Protection Program.

The mouse must surmise that we are not compatible. It gets back at me by refusing to acknowledge my clicking.

"Why don't you *click?*" my husband/teacher barks. "I did." "Let me do it!" Click. Nothing. Click, Click. Nothing. Then click—and it works. Unlike a dog, a mouse will not always perform on command—at least not for the lady of the house, who can be expert at clicking with children—but doesn't click with a mouse.

I am initiated into the dark mysteries of online and writing e-mail letters. Suddenly—INTRUSION! "Do you want to *save*?" A neighbor has come to visit with her six-year-old grandson. I babble out my ignorance, "How do I SAVE?"

The boy goes to the computer, touches the mouse. Voila! My work is saved by a six-year-old child I hadn't known could even read.

As I work, one of Florida's severe rainstorms is pelting down. Thunder and lightning often cause power outages, so perhaps if….

FOUND—A DAUGHTER
As told to Evelyn Goldstein

I had been feeling particularly despondent all that day and came home from work more depressed than usual.

It was only two months since my son Barry died. I hated the apartment. I was still not used to the quiet and the loneliness.

I picked up my mail. There were several bills, a picture postcard from a friend and a letter from a Ruth Laramy. The name struck me like a bullet. My fingers trembled as I tore open the letter.

Dear Mrs. Holt: I have been able to get in touch with you because my mother gave our lawyer permission to tell me what I wanted to know about you. I will call you Thursday at 8 p.m.

Sincerely,

Ruth Laramy.

For the moment, I could scarcely breathe. The letter was from my daughter, whom I had given up for adoption seventeen years ago!

My gaze went to a framed picture of my son Barry. Barry was the reason I had given up my second child. Barry's learning difficulties and bizarre behavior problems stemmed from a psychotic state. He was schizophrenic. We had hoped he would outgrow his problems, but he did not. And his hostile and destructive tendencies worsened. No amount of affection and care that my husband and I gave him could convince my son that we were not continually plotting against him. He became sulkily childish, or brutally aggressive—screaming accusations—or throwing things about.

In the beginning, when Barry was still very young and before my husband David and I became aware of the true nature of our son's condition, we had planned to have another child. But I did not conceive. As Barry became worse each year, we became relieved that I was not pregnant.

When I was close to forty years old and Barry was fourteen, I found myself pregnant. I was in my fifth month of pregnancy when my husband died suddenly of a massive heart attack. He left so many debts incurred by Barry's illness that I could not make ends meet. Barry and I were evicted from the apartment. I had to move in with my parents, who only had three small rooms. How could I bring another child into such a crowded and troubled home, particularly with a violent sibling?

One particularly bad day my son Barry became so abusive that he struck my parents and me. The neighbors called the police because of the severe disturbance. That is when I decided on the course of action I had to take: as soon as I had the baby, I would give her up for adoption.

I confided in my obstetrician, who was sympathetic. He advised me to think this over, but if I was still determined to go ahead, he knew of a fine couple who wanted a child desperately. They would give my baby a good home. They would also take care of all the medical and hospital expenses and would give me money, as well.

Much as I needed the money, I refused it. I did not want to feel I was selling my baby, but I did want my child to have a healthy, normal family. It was an act of love.

All during those next few months I prayed for a miracle. That fall I gave birth to a healthy baby girl. I lied to my family and friends, saying my baby had been still-born. My mother kept insisting, "How? Why? You were doing so well. What happened? We must make arrangements for a funeral!"

"*No! No funeral.*" My voice had risen to a high pitch. I felt myself close to hysteria. "The hospital will take care of everything. Please, Mother, I want it that way. Don't talk about it anymore." Seeing how agitated I had become, she dropped the subject. Perhaps, deep down, she was relieved. Those next few months were the hardest. When I went to sign the final adoption papers, I begged the lawyer to tell me the name of my baby's adoptive parents. He refused. He assured me that she was well and living in a fine home with the best of everything. I had to be satisfied with that.

In the years that followed, Barry got worse. He had to be institutionalized time and again. I kept assuring myself that I had done the right thing by giving my daughter up for adoption. Was I trying to justify what I had done? Perhaps. Religion suddenly became a way of life for me. I prayed for guidance. Prayer was my great comfort.

Adoption laws began to change. Organizations were being formed to help adoptees and their biological parents meet. I joined such an organization and with their help was able to find out the name of my child's adoptive parents. They were a Dr. and Mrs. Laramy. And my daughter's name was Ruth. That was how I recognized her name when I received her letter.

Barry was in and out of institutions. He had begun to complain of constant pains. After many tests, the doctors insisted the pains were imaginary. Not so, said Barry. The pains were real, agonizing and unbearable. It broke my heart to watch him suffer. He started to drink, to pop pills and he became even more antagonistic if reprimanded him. I was at my wit's end.

Fortunately, I had a job. That and my steadfast belief that God would help, saved my sanity. Then, about two months ago, I returned from work to find Barry dead from a combination of pills and liquor. Gone was the memory of the bad times. All I could think of was the fact that my son was dead. I cried and cried. My parents had long since died. I had no one. I was alone.

Then, like an answer from God, I received Ruth's letter. I felt that I was no longer alone. I was filled with joy. Then reality set in. I did not really have a daughter. After all, I had given her up for adoption. Would she accept my reasons for doing that? I became panic-stricken. My hands felt damp. Why did she want to see me now, after all these years? I dreaded recriminations.

I agonized through those next few days until Thursday when she telephoned. I kept tight control of myself when the phone rang and her sweet, pleasant voice came over the wire, "This is Ruth Laramy." My heart beat fast. "Yes, I know," I said. "I was waiting for your call."

"Then, you do want to see me?"

"Yes. Oh, yes!" Was I shouting? I calmed down. Her voice spoke again. "Would you like to meet somewhere? Or would you rather I come to your home?"

"Please come here." We made an appointment for the following day.

That next morning, I waited anxiously, pacing the floor. The doorbell finally rang. I opened the door and there she was, a pretty, blond girl with the same facial features as my late husband, except that she had big, brown eyes like mine. She seemed shy. I tried to put her at ease and finally succeeded. I had prepared a light lunch and, over coffee, we became better acquainted. It was then I learned that her adoptive father was dead and that she had truly adored him. She was attending college and planning a career in law.

I asked if I could meet her mother. I wanted to thank her for having brought Ruth up to be such a fine person. But Ruth did not think this was a good idea, since her mother was not well. Perhaps at a later date.

Now Ruth began to ask questions about her brother. I told her about Barry and she accepted my explanation with sympathy. She was interested in knowing about her father. I assured her that he had been a good and kind man. I told her I would not interfere between her and her adoptive mother, but that I would like her friendship. She agreed to this.

We parted, promising to see each other again. We embraced. Maybe next time we will kiss. I hope so. Finding my daughter again, knowing she is normal and healthy and grown into a fine person has, at last, given me peace of mind. I realize that the terribly difficult decision to give Ruth up, so she might have a chance for a better life, was a necessary and right choice.

For helping me set my baby on the path best for her, I thank you, God.

FRIENDSHIP'S SIGNPOSTS

As a New York City Elementary School teacher for over twenty years, I have watched many children's friendships blossom and wane, or remain steadfast.

Friendships in the public schools can be rewarding experiences and bind chums closer than identical twins. When the tie is strained or broken, the child can hardly concentrate on anything else. Studies may become impaired and test-marks fall. Whether I have taught sixth-grade or third-grade, I have made it a practice each term to tack up a manila envelope on the supply closet door, where the children can put a note for my attention.

Often, appeals come scrawled on a piece of paper yanked out of a spiral note-book, or scribbled on a teeny scrap, wadded up tight so no one will have the patience to open it. I have the patience. Often these nervously written wads are poignant: "Jenny is writing notes to my friends that they shouldn't talk to me." "Linda takes everybody's things. She goes into desks." "Danny tries to look up girl's dresses when we have to wear skirts to Assembly. The girls say we should all beat up on him after school, but my mother won't let me fight. Can you help me?" "Ann won't stay my friend because I get higher marks. My daddy won't let me stop studying."

When you have taught hundreds of children, you cannot remember all of them, but many of them remain in your mind long years after—not necessarily because they are the brightest, or the most popular, but because they have some innate need, or lovely warmth. They have become someway special.

I knew about Lori before she came to my third-grade class. She was a trans-feree from another school on the Open Enrollment Plan, which permits minority group parents to choose the school they wish their child to attend. Then, the child becomes a "bused-in" student because buses take them from their neighbor-hood to out-of-neighborhood schools.

The records arrived before Lori. Along with her medical, scholastic and per-sonal history came an envelope marked "Anecdotal". My heart sank. Anecdotals are on-the-spot memos written by staff members when troublesome children cause problems. They are dated and the incident is recorded without opinion or judgment on the teacher's part.

Lori's anecdotal was one long summary by various teachers, aides and resource persons about lateness, truancy, fighting, biting, discourtesy to adults, defiance to authority, etc. The one incident I particularly noted was that she refused to stand during the Pledge of Allegiance; also, that she spat at any one who tried to reason with her. I considered all this. It would be important to seat her with the proper desk-mate. Should it be Karlyn, a street-wise girl who was a born leader? Should it be shy Amy, or quiet Jill?

Lori came in late the next morning, not because the bus was delayed, but because she stayed in the school-yard rather than come to class. A monitor brought her to the door and I stepped into the hall for the moment it took to accept the admittance form. The monitor left. I smiled at Lori, "Welcome to our Class 3-113." She watched me warily. She was tall for an eight-year-old with beautiful wide-set, dark eyes and skin like warm, brown suede.

"Oh, Lori," I cried out impulsively. "You are beautiful," and I hugged her, kissing that lovely cheek. Surprise flickered in her face and she relaxed a bit. I drew her into the classroom and said, "Class, this is your new friend Lori. Now which one of you will show her where to hang up her jacket?" A dozen hands went up. I chose one small, eagerly waving hand. "Dezi," I called, "Please help Lori and be her partner."

It was a spontaneous decision when I saw Dezi's frantically raised fingers, waving like an S.O.S. Lori heard snickers—ill concealed—and quickly squelched at my stern glare. I threw a sidelong look at Lori. "Lori," I whispered for her hearing only, "please take care of Dezi, too."

Lori was startled, but in the hours to follow she would understand. Dezi was slow and prone to such deep daydreaming that she rarely concentrated on instructions. Next day was to be lower grade assembly day. It was to be our turn to choose color guard for the month of October. "Lori, I would like you to be the bearer of the American flag tomorrow. You will be the one to call out the order to: "Salute. Pledge." I chose Dezi from amongst the six guards. Dezi was the shortest girl in class. Lori was the tallest. I wanted Dezi to stand as close to Lori as possible, so I assigned positions—shortest radiating to tallest out from center bearer.

Lori bore the flag up to the platform and gave the Pledge commands in a proud ringing tone. She kept that job for the entire month. That year—and as far as I know, in future years—there was not a single disrespectful incident from Lori in the auditorium.

As for Dezi, she found a fierce protector in Lori. I had sensed in our newcomer a need, not only for recognition, but for achievement. Dezi was always chosen last for team games and never included in the schoolyard camaraderie. Lori changed all that. When she made it clear in blunt words that Dezi was to be part of all activities, that was how it was. In time, Dezi gained confidence and earned her own acceptance because of Lori's staunch backing.

In class, Lori guided Dezi whenever she daydreamed through instructions. Dezi's daydreams diminished. Her work improved. For her part, Dezi gave Lori the admiration and respect she had never had before. Lori's fights, lateness, absences grew less and less. By the end of term she was receiving gold stars for punctuality, excellent attendance and conduct.

Dezi rose from below-grade level to on-grade level. This strangely matched pair remained friends all of their lives, despite divergent futures. Dezi married a career Army man, had children and traveled wherever the military assignment led.

Lori became a supervisor of computer personnel and commanded a superlative salary with bright prospects.

They had given to and taken from, each other, what each one needed: caring, sharing, thoughtfulness, respect; All those "doings for" had turned into love. And those, in the final analysis, are the signposts to friendship along the paths of our lives.

HAVEN'T WE MET BEFORE?

It was by sheer accident that Margo saw the lettering on the glass of the office door:

CREIGHBAR & STANDER
Attorneys at Law

She had mistakenly left the elevator on the eighth floor, when she should have gotten off at the sixth. Without her eyeglasses, the numbers looked similar. She simply must forego her vanity, she thought and either wear glasses or get contact lenses. Her eyes had grown worse since her 50th birthday.

Standing before the door, she knew that this was the office of William Creighbar, who had been her best beau in high school. They had been such a "steady" twosome that it was hard to remember how their graduation and subsequent attendance at different colleges had so totally separated them.

When she had met Gary Aimes in the biology lab—where he helped her dissect the grasshopper she "absolutely could not touch"—it was easy to go from dating, to engagement, to marriage.

She had heard from William Creighbar that he was seeing an education major at the university where he was studying law. It was not long before he, too, was married. After that, she and William lost contact. She did hear, from mutual friends, that William had a son and daughter. She imagined the same sources had let William know that she was childless, pursuing a career in public relations management and being very successful at it.

Soon after their twentieth year of marriage her husband Gary had suffered a heart attack and was "gone" within a week. She was grateful for her demanding position, which kept her as busy at the office, as at home. It saved her from the loneliness of suddenly finding herself part of the "singles" set.

She might never have given any thought to William had she not seen his name on the glass door. Suddenly shy, she could not bring herself to enter the office. What could she say to the receptionist? "Hello, I'm an old flame of Mr. Creighbar. Can you tell me, is he still married?"

Just the thought of that embarrassed her. She could not believe this was really her, hurrying back down the corridor to the elevator—retreating.

In her job she was a self-assured woman. She took measures that were needed with a surety and confidence that had brought her promotion after promotion, rising from supervisor to executive. Yet, she found herself unable to face the challenge of meeting an old friend face-to-face.

She had changed with the years. He certainly would not recognize this stylish woman with the elegant ash-silver hairdo. She had been a fluffy blond when they had dated. Her face had been round and pink, not thin and hollow-cheeked as dieting and age had turned it. Still chastising herself for not opening the door of the law office, she took the elevator down to the sixth floor.

She completed her business of setting up the trade-show for next month in Atlanta. It took several hours, so she telephoned her office to say she would not be back that afternoon. She needed to get home and get control of some new emotions that had been wakened in her by encountering the name that had meant so much in her youth.

When she had to face the next day at work, she found her mind dwelling on the prospect of meeting William. She found herself thumbing through the telephone book to find the listing and dial the number of his office.

When the receptionist answered, she said there was a planned business party and needed to know the first name of Mrs. Creighbar.

"There is no Mrs. Creighbar," the telephone operator supplied. "They have been divorced for years." Divorced. Her heart soared. Now they were both free. She could go to him and reintroduce herself. Surely, it would not be so hard to pick up again—despite the many years between. She paid particular attention to her dress the next day. During her lunch hour, she took a taxi to the building that William's firm occupied.

It was almost another stroke of luck when she walked into the marbled lobby and there he was, William Creighbar himself. He stood for a moment, looking toward the entrance doors, as though expecting someone to come through. She marveled how little life had changed him. He had always kept himself physically fit. She had no trouble recognizing him. Would he find her as recognizable? She hastened toward him, hand extended. "Will. Will Creighbar!"

He turned and looked at her. She felt herself getting giddy. The years had been unbelievably kind to him. Oh, certainly he was older than in their high school days, but nothing as mature as she. No wonder he did not recognize her.

Usually she was a very contained person. She could not understand why she suddenly felt herself turning coy, saying playfully, "Don't you know me?"

Again the blank stare. She felt so frustrated. If only he would show some slight recognition she would not feel so ancient. She felt her face coloring with heat. It made her cry out, not as much in anger as in irritation, "How could you have forgotten me so completely?" Surely, there must still be some resemblance, however slight, in her features to the girl he once had loved.

"Excuse me," he murmured, looking over her head. "There is someone I must see."

He rushed past her. She turned and stared, uncomprehending. A uniformed nurse was pushing a wheelchair through the door. Seated in the chair was a white-haired man with drooping face, who had obviously suffered a major stroke. He was trying to lift his head, trying in vain to speak. William Creighbar ran to him. "It's good to see you. How do you feel?"

The older man peered up with impaired memory, struggling to recognize William who cried, "It's me—Willie, your son."

KISS OF DEPTH

A kiss is just a kiss,

A sigh is just a sigh,

These sentimental things apply,

As time goes by.

This was a tune popular when a four-letter word usually meant love. At that time, a kiss was truly just a kiss. Today, it is a tongue sandwich.

The open-mouth kiss is very "in"—if you'll forgive the pun. This is the result of a generation weaned on Big Macs, Whoppers, heroes, subs and medical practitioners who instruct, "Open wide! This won't hurt a bit!"

Our stars of the screen—beautiful, handsome, charismatic—regard each other tenderly. He gazes into her eyes, his feelings soulful, warm and adoring. Gently he strokes her cheek and meets her amorous, smitten regard. She reaches up and draws his head down.

I sigh. I am a deep-rooted sentimentalist. I smile nostalgically. How charming. How touching....

Wrong word!

Like gouramis, they open their mouths and kiss. Their heads move from side to side. They lick. They nibble. Their tongues check out teeth, palates, gums—all without use of instruments.

Suddenly! A frenzy of motion. Unlacing, untying, unclasping, unzipping ... Clothes go flying all about. A shirt, a blouse, hit the camera. Scene goes blank. When the garments fall to the floor, the camera is operational again. The lovers are on the bed and all over each other. Without a halt they explore each other's mouths.

I, the watcher, being a mother—in the old-fashioned meaning of the word, have studied the Mother's Code. First commandment—WORRY. What if, in the heat of the moment, one bites the other? He might be wearing a condom for protection. But, in this case, he could wear condoms in layers atop each other and not prevent AIDS.

So where does the responsibility lie? With the audience? Partly. They could write letters and make phone calls. But audiences are notoriously passive. The actors? Hardly. They make their living by performing. The writers, directors, producers? Yes, to a great extent. They're out for the ratings. They have apparently forgotten that for decades the screen portrayed sex scenes by innuendo and the appeal of those classics has still not diminished.

The sponsors? Now we come to the heart of the problem. With a wave of their financial wands they could create an ethical climate for audiences. Then why aren't they doing this? Have such mighty conglomerates as General Mills, the cola companies, the fast food super-magnates found they can make a mint out of open-mouth kissing? Will a titillated audience be turned on? More likely, we will be turned in—to our refrigerators for snacks after watching the nibbling on screen.

In the bedroom, the choice is private. On the big screen, it becomes public business. When you come down to the nitty-gritty (or just the gritty) whose choice earns the plaque for passing the kiss of depth on to our future culture? And how, in the final analysis, do the young folk regard it? As a lesson to learn and emulate? As passion? Or—as hunger?

LET'S TALK TURKEY

Thanksgiving has a special meaning to our family which goes back many years to our youth after World War I. We were very poor and lived in a tenement in the Williamsburg section of Brooklyn. Papa was a cutter in the garment industry, but the work was seasonal. There was no unemployment insurance in those days, so Mama budgeted each paycheck for those lean days of lay-offs.

Since our parents came from Europe, they were not familiar with such an American holiday as Thanksgiving, but we four children learned about it in school. In the classrooms we were told the story of the landing at Plymouth Rock and the bitterness of winter for the Pilgrims. We learned how the Indians helped with the harvest and with hunting of the game and how Pilgrims and Indians feasted together, giving thanks to God for the bountiful harvest.

We children loved the story. What we did not love was the knowledge that all over America, children were sitting down with relatives and friends, eating the traditional Thanksgiving fare—turkey, sweet potatoes, cranberry sauce. And in our house there could be no such feasting.

"Will you be having a Thanksgiving dinner?" our classmates asked.

"Of course," we lied loftily. And we knew we would lie about having eaten so much, we were ready to burst. It was not that Mama and Papa would have been against banqueting as others did. It was simply that we had no money for such luxuries. Our family had never tasted turkey. We only knew from the few fortunate friends, whose parents were comparatively affluent, that turkey was more delicious than anything in the world.

"Couldn't we get a small turkey?"

They did not grow small turkeys. A twenty-pound bird or larger, was average in those days. And who could afford twenty pounds of bird? We tried to be understanding of the financial situation, but children want to be like other children. Having a traditional Thanksgiving dinner became an obsession. We were good children and understanding of our parents' problems. But we were, basically, children.

We suggested all sorts of ways a turkey could be purchased cheap. Mama would simply shake her head. She had given up trying to explain why we couldn't do it this year. "Maybe next year," she held out. But we hadn't had it last year, or the year before. We just had to have it this year, or conclude that never, never in our lives would we be truly Americanized if we did not eat turkey on Thanksgiving.

Suddenly, a miracle happened. There was a big sale on sweet potatoes at twenty pounds to the bag. Mama dragged the bag of sweet potatoes up the three flights of stairs, along with loose cranberries, somewhat crushed by heavier produce and sold at an especially low price.

So, two-thirds of the traditional Thanksgiving dinner was already in our house. And it was two days before Thanksgiving. All of us fell to peeling the potatoes with Mama, while urging her to buy the turkey. Our friends had told us their mothers had already ordered them at the poultry store where they were on final sale since the holiday was almost here! Mama went downstairs to haggle with the poultry man. "We will have turkey this Thanksgiving," she came back to tell us.

What anticipation!

Mama said that because turkey was so special and because she had never made one before, we children were to stay out of the kitchen while she was preparing dinner. She was going to do something she had rarely had to do before; she was going to follow a recipe.

We were just as happy to be banished from the kitchen. When Mama wanted errands run, we hurried to obey: "Bring me carrots for the soup." Or, "Prepare the table with the best china and silver." Not the everyday odds and ends from the pushcart, but out of Mama's marriage dowry in the china closet.

The great afternoon of Thursday, Thanksgiving Day, arrived at last. Papa, like the King, at the head of the table, listened while we told him the story of Thanksgiving. Mama brought out apple juice, with chipped ice from the ice-box to make it tangy cold and spread it further. Apple cider was unaffordable. We were just as happy with the juice.

The cranberry sauce came out in another wedding gift—a crystal compote bowl with matching crystal ladling spoon.

At last, the turkey. On a platter, it arrived, with a glaze of golden honey over it. With bulging eyes we stared as Mama set the platter in front of Papa and gave him a whetted knife for the carving. Papa studied the bird. We sat there, staring at it, scarcely breathing. Papa said, "Bobby, do you want the white meat or the dark?"

Bobby, not taking his eyes off our turkey said, "Wh—wh—white, Papa, please."

Papa flourished the knife and sliced into the breast area while Bobby lifted his plate to receive his portion. "And you, Sammy?" Papa asked me.

I could hardly answer. My voice seemed to squeak in my throat. I tried twice, before saying, "White, please, Papa." Again the flourish. I passed my plate. Then Papa turned to Helen.

"The drumstick. I'd like the drumstick."

Papa frowned, concentrating on the best way to sever the drumstick. "Be careful of the bones," he cautioned and said the same to Fran when she, too, requested a drumstick.

"I'll be careful," Fran promised.

"Mama," Bob said when he pushed his empty plate away. "This is the most special Thanksgiving dinner in America." Mama looked across the table. There were tears in her eyes. "Next year...." she began to say.

But Papa said, "Next year is unimportant. It is this Thanksgiving we will always remember."

With tears falling from her eyes, Mama had to smile as she looked at the big platter which earlier had held the sweet potatoes she had cooked and mashed and shaped into the form of a roasted turkey. On Monday, back at school, we would, in all honesty, be able to tell that "Our Mama serves Thanksgiving turkey like nobody else in America."

LOAF ME OR KNEAD ME

Nobody likes to be taken for granted. Neither does bread. Oh, don't give me that wide-eyed look and scream, "BREAD!" Yes, bread. I ask you to think—when did you ever treat bread with kindness? You see it in a wrapper, you squeeze it. Since Charmin commercials appeared, you wouldn't dare squeeze toilet paper. But do you think twice about squeezing bread, perhaps poking a finger into a roll? Nobody does.

What about pinching off bits? What about tearing it into pieces? What about rolling nips absent-mindedly into little balls while you are talking about something important like, "Who's your plumber?" Some people care. They butter up to bread. Not so the bread-scalders who don't even hesitate to dunk a wedge into steaming hot coffee.

Bread is not inanimate like a rock, you know. It breathes. It rises. It crumples. With rich ingredients going into it, it doubles in bulk, even as you and I.

Bread is called the staff of life, but is not used for walking, or pole-vaulting or jousting. In biblical psalms they don't say, "Thy rod and thy bagel, they comfort me."

If the Lord had tried to rout the enemy by throwing pita or sopapillas instead of smiting them with wrath, the most that could happen is that they would have been vanquished by obesity.

Bread is inoffensive. It is not a weapon. You can't wield it with a threatening gesture—point a breadstick and command, "Stick 'em up." Because bread is harmless we take it for granted. We pay more attention to splitting the atom, or cracking the sound barrier. Those make the news.

Would the New York Times sell newspapers if it headlined, "BAKERS' DOZEN THROWS COMPUTERS INTO CONFUSION?" A kind gesture, like giving an extra roll for every twelve purchased, could catapult the world into panic. Computers could not understand it. Twelve is twelve. When twelve becomes thirteen they'd blow—outages all over Earth. "BAKERS START WORLD WAR III."

The first breads were unleavened—the original pita and matzahs were baked on a hot stone. We can assume that some caveman's kid, playing the shell game with friends, had to cast away the nutmeats and flung them into Mama's dough by accident. And so, nut bread was born. We assume that Man, being innovative, felt that if nuts could add taste, why not berries?

Maybe they even tried chopped rawhide. You can imagine one Indian Chief saying to the other, "Let's go to Joe's for some kick-a-poo-mead. He sets out a basket of free pemmican sticks."

In the same accidental way, yeast molds were discovered to cause the flour concoctions to rise. In rising, the bread developed a softer, more palatable texture. That's when calories came into being.

More recently, in our diet-conscious society, pita has come into its own. So, here we are, an ultra-sophisticated civilization, casting laboratories out into space and information missiles out of our galaxy. But, in our eating of bread, we have returned full circle to the flat flour and water mixture of our prehistoric ancestors.

America used to treat bread with respect. Mornings were given over to toast. Lunches were dominated by sandwiches. No dinner was elegant without a basket of assorted fresh rolls.

Suddenly the scene has changed. Bread is no longer dominant. As Rodney Dangerfield says, "It gets no respect."

Why? Because the French Queen, Marie Antoinette imperiously decreed, "Let them eat cake." And today America is romancing—the croissant.

A CHRISTMAS DOG TALE

Christmas doesn't mean much to me. My name is Hobo and I am a two-year-old dog of such mixed breed that even the most competent veterinarian could never accurately guess my lineage. I've been pretty much on the streets most of my life and about the only thing Christmas means to me is that I can scrounge for more and better delicacies in the garbage cans during this holiday season.

I am not complaining, you understand. In my lifetime I've had one or two owners, but the adoptions were short-lived. They usually happened when some kid would see me and begin to pet me and say something like, "Hey, Boy. Hey, nice feller." And when I would lift my face for petting, I would be encouraged to follow him or her, home, where it was announced, "Look, Ma, look what I found. Can I keep him? Can I? Please, oh, please …"

Either the answer would be a firm, sharp, "NO!" and out I'd go. Or a hesitant, "No," and then the triumphant child could get me inside the house. Then, usually an old towel, or used blanket would be spread in a corner. Those kind humans gave me water and some food.

If I was lucky to get into a place where a pet had once been, out would come some kibble—definitely not fresh—but, hey! better than some garbage fare.

Then would come the trial period. I would go to the door, hoping bathroom privileges would be provided. The adults would ignore me, "because he's your dog," they would remind their child. "You wanted him. You've got to walk him."

But kids are pretty much all alike—they want a pet, but not responsibility. So there I would be, at the door, waiting and hoping. If it would be an overlong wait, I'd offer up a little whimper.

Usually ignored.

I'd wait some more. Then, if things were getting urgent, I'd make a little bark. If lucky, the grown-up would take me out on some make-shift rope tied around my neck, sometimes pretty choking. But it made me do my thing quickly and get back inside until the next test of bladder endurance. Sometimes an adult would open the door, let me out and shut the door, hoping I'd take off to parts unknown and I'd hear the adult voice say to the child, "The dog ran away!" A sure signal for me to amble out onto the streets again.

I have learned to be as invisible as possible because there are humans who are not nice to animals, especially to strays. Some yell at you to get away. But some try to catch you to get kicks out of mistreating you. The best thing to do when a human is around is to slink off and not stay around to see his intentions.

But—the lucky times are when you encounter a human who really, truly wants a pet.

And that's what happened to me. A few days ago, the temperature went down, down, down and the snows piled up, up, up. I just could not find any sort of shelter from the cold along the icy wall. Even though I found some discarded newspapers and lay on them for protection from the icy pavement, they soon got sodden and were no safeguard against the freezing ground.

I just knew this was THE END! I was too cold to move and ice had packed into my paw pads. Although I was near a housing development, none of the inside steam-heat reached the alley where I lay.

"Goodbye, Hobo," I thought. An answer came. "Hello, fellow! You're in bad shape, aren't you?" And, bending over me was Santa Claus. Red suit, red and white hat, white beard and all. I never believed in Santa Claus. Never before. But here he was, a tall, strong man, lifting me in his arms and carrying me into the big building—the warm, steam-heated building. There was a doorman. He peered into the bushy face of the man who held me and said, "Hey, Mr. Manners, is that you in the Santa suit?"

"It sure is me. I'm playing Santa at our big family dinner. You remember Scooter, our dog who died last month? He was also a stray, but we had him for fourteen years. And we all missed him and missed a dog around the house. Well, I just found a replacement—a Christmas present to my family. Meet Hobo." So that's how come I was adopted on Christmas Eve.

And that's why I now believe in Santa Claus.

CANDLES IN THE SNOW

The Mother loved to dance. She was nineteen years old. She would lift Baby out of the crib and waltz her around the small tenement apartment, singing as she went. Baby was eight months old and would cuddle her head against the mother's neck and gurgle with delight.

In the apartment across the hall, the man would listen. He was twenty-eight years old and remembered when he and his wife and five year old daughter had sung and danced in their larger apartment in another part of town. But that was before a drunk driver had smashed into their car, killing his wife and daughter and leaving him with his leg in a metal brace up to the knee.

He had moved out of his larger apartment, clear across town to this older, less expensive place. At that time his lawsuit had not been settled. Now it was—leaving him with a generous amount that would keep him comfortable for the rest of his life. He would have moved to better quarters, but Mother and Baby and the boyfriend had moved next door and the Man decided not to make any changes in his life. Not yet.

The boyfriend was also young and had no patience for Baby when she cried. Like the mother, he enjoyed good times and when they danced and made love he was quite content to stay around. But when Baby cried he would get upset.

"Can't you keep that kid quiet!" he would shout.

The mother would try, but babies fret and all the soothing and petting and walking around did not help. So, one day, the boyfriend left the house, vowing never to return. The man would listen to the mother's sobbing and hear Baby crying in her crib. For a while he stayed, sitting in his chair, his body growing tenser as he listened.

Finally, he lifted himself out of the chair and went across the hall. He knocked on the door. The sobbing from inside was choked down. She must have wiped her eyes hastily. Perhaps she patted her hair. She called out, "Who is it?"

"I'm your neighbor. Can I help?" The door opened. She was holding Baby, who was still fretting and sobbing.

The man held out his strong arms. "I used to have a daughter." She looked into his face. His expression told her much. She gave the crying Baby to him and stood quiet as he came into the room, holding Baby and whispering, "There, there. It's all right. You're fine. You're safe...."

Baby gave a little hiccough that ended the tearful spasm and laid her head against his cheek, soothed to quiet contentment by his murmured assurances. In a little while she was fast asleep and the mother took her and laid her in her crib.

She turned. "Thank you," she said. Then, as a hesitant afterthought, "Can I get you some coffee? Tea?"

"Either would be fine." She made instant coffee for both and they sat at the kitchen table.

"I only have some Arrowroot cookies," she apologized. "For the baby, you know."

"Just the coffee is fine. I try to keep trim, to keep pressure off this leg." She asked about it and he told her, briefly, unemotionally and asked her, "What about you?"

"I left my parents' farm when I knew I was pregnant." The father of the child came along, being young and anticipating fun in a big city. And it had been fun for a while. But, after Baby arrived and their money dwindled and he had to get a dishwashing job in a saloon, the glamour faded.

"You need to get a job," the man advised her.

"How can I leave the baby alone?"

"I can baby-sit."

She didn't really know. She did love her child. She had never left her before. But there seemed no alternative. At the man's urging, she ventured forth that very morning. She came back in late afternoon and told him, "I did get a job." She had been hired by one of the fast-food chains and her training period would begin next day.

And so it began. When the mother left for work, the man would care for the baby. And when she returned, he would have food ready and he would return to his apartment, while she remained in hers. On weekends they stayed by themselves. She appeared to have a shyness about the great debt she owed him, which she felt she never could repay. He had an innate respect for her private life. Then the boyfriend returned.

The man listened at his door, hearing their laughter and the sounds of music as they danced and then worse—the silence in the darkened apartment. But when the baby began to cry, he would hear the boyfriend order, "Let her cry! God's sakes do you have to pick her up every time she makes a sound!"

But the mother did. The boyfriend would grow angrier and angrier, shouting louder and louder, "Let her cry!"

One day he struck the mother! The man across the hall heard the sound of flesh against flesh. He heard the sharp cry of pain and outrage! He lifted himself out of his chair, on his powerful hands. He dragged his metal-braced leg across the hall and flung open the door.

In the tableau he beheld the mother, holding her cheek where there was a red mark from the blow. The man asked, "Do you want him to stay?"

She shook her head. "No," she said.

The man took the boyfriend by the shoulders, spun him about and shoved him out the door. "Don't come back! *Ever!*" The boyfriend, without a word, took off, never to return. The mother was crying.

"I'm sorry," the man said. "If you want him back...."

"No!" she was definite. "We don't need him."

The man was not sure whether the 'we' included him, until she held out her hand and took his. She led him to the window. On the sill was a little silver nine-branched electric candelabra. She gave the middle one a slight twist and orange light came on.

Then she lit the first candle of the row. "It is the first night of our celebration of Chanukah. Each night we light another candle."

"Why do you celebrate Chanukah?" he asked.

"Chanukah means 'dedication.' It is a celebration of religious freedom. Judah Maccabee defeated the Syrians. When the Jews came to their temple the Syrians had destroyed it. All the holy oil was defiled, except one lamp with enough oil for one day. The miracle happened when the flame stayed lit for eight days. That's why Chanukah is observed for eight days.

The sound of singing began from outside. They looked through the window. Snow had begun to fall. Carolers had gathered. When the singers saw the menorah, they conferred. Then they began to sing the joyful little Chanukah song, "I Have A Little Dreidel." The mother ran back to the kitchen table and snatched up a net of golden, foil-covered chocolates. Opening the window, she cast it out for the singers, who smiled their thanks at the sweet golden gift.

When they finished the Chanukah song, they began to sing, "Jingle Bells." The man smiled and took the mother's hand in his, clasping it firmly.

The night was filled with white snow flurries and with the orange flame of the Chanukah candles. The carolers sang of love, joy and tolerance toward all—which is as it should be—at Chanukah, at Christmas and—all through the year.

CASH AND CARRY

Officer Joe Brown was convinced the Cash and Carry general store was a drug front. It was just too respectable a place in the midst of the dilapidated old tenements with graffiti-ed walls and broken, marked-up sidewalks.

Sara and Tom Sims, the kindly, grandparent-like proprietors gave scrupulous attention to their business. Every morning they opened sharply at eight and every evening they closed at five. In between, they courteously waited on customers and during any lull, folded merchandise, replaced goods on hangers and shelves and ceaselessly polished the glass window, door and counters.

On sunny days they swept the sidewalk outside several times and mopped the patterned parquet linoleum floor whenever it was scuffed by shoes or boots. They were most meticulous about the counter holding the candy and snack displays, near the cash register toward the front of the store. "Food must be kept sanitary," they reminded when a grimy hand would reach for the dome covered doughnuts, where an index card advised, "Let us get it for you, The Proprietors," Then the chosen doughnut would be taken out on waxed paper in which it was wrapped, put into a paper bag and given to the customer.

The four-foot, glass meat counter was also scrupulously washed inside and out, then polished with glass cleaner until it sparkled. The racks where ladies blouses hung were dusted by pushing the hangers to one end, running a clean rag over the metal bar and reversing the procedure. The same was the case with the men's shirts on the next rack and the toys on shelves nearest the door.

The inventory was not big, but seemed sufficient for the clientele who had little spending money, along with food stamps.

When Joe had voiced his suspicions to his captain, the man looked up from behind his paper-littered desk with astonishment. Like everyone in that district, the Sims were regarded as the bright spot in a bleak horizon.

"Joe, get the bad guys. I'm not assigning any stakeout of that Cash & Carry store."

Joe couldn't shake off his hunch, so he used his own time on weekends, holidays and punch-out time. There was nothing he could ever put his finger on, as he watched people go into the store, come out with bags, or wrapped parcels. Once he even drove over in his own car, out of uniform and went inside to case the joint. Nothing abnormal.

He followed some customers several times, pretending to bump into them and make them drop their packages. Apologizing and helping retrieve the fallen items, he would only find a shirt, or child's toy, some snack such as a bag of pretzels and wrapped Baby Ruth or Hershey Bar. Sometimes the waxed paper wrapped cuts of meat might have fallen on the dirty pavement, but the Sims had wrapped them carefully and taped them with freezer tape and the price on them was plainly evident.

All it proved, Joe discovered, was that the prices charged were quite reasonable—especially on the days when they put a sign in the front window, SALE TODAY! and merchandise was discounted 10%.

Unable to find any conclusive evidence, Joe decided to confront the Sims and startle them into betraying their guilt.

That night, just before the store closed at five, Joe waited outside and as soon as the last customer left and the Sims began to darken the store, preparing to close up, Joe went inside.

"I'm a police officer." He flipped open his identity badge. "I've been watching you for a long time. I know what you are doing."

The two looked at him, wide-eyed. When they exchanged glances with each other, Joe caught the guilty looks. A rush of triumph swept through him. "Aha!" He had been right all along.

Pressing on, he cried, "I know you've been *selling drugs!*"

Joe was not prepared for the look of utter blankness with which they returned his stare. He was staggered to realize they had not the foggiest notion of what he was accusing them.

Sara Sims was so righteously indignant that Joe realized she was definitely not involved in drug dealing. If not drugs, what?

"Officer," she cried, "drugs are illegal! We would never dream of selling drugs. Why, we could lose our business—even—even go to jail! No! No! we would never deal in drugs—never, never!"

Her husband—equally shaken at such a thought—said, "Drugs is a dirty business. We keep everything clean here. Everyone knows that. Our customers know our food is fresh. Our cakes and cookies are delivered the day we sell them. And if they aren't all sold we wrap up what's left and bring it to the soup kitchen at the corner so the hungry people can eat."

His wife assured, "Everyone knows our food is fresh—especially our meat! Our meat is fresh cut every day."

The last thing Joe heard just before he died, was Jim Sims vowing with absolute truthfulness, "fresh cut—and—on the hoof!"

DADDY, WHY DID YOU HAVE TO DIE?

Down from the vaulted, stained glass windows came muted rays of early sunlight to touch my husband's face as he lay in the satin-lined casket. My nineteen-year old son Bob held my arm protectively and mourners came up to offer soft condolences, to which I nodded tearfully. I hardly heard what they said as they filed off to take seats in the memorial chapel, which was filling up fast.

My thoughts were with Myra, my fourteen-year old daughter. She sat silent and frozen on the front bench. Her eyes never left the casket where her daddy lay. I realized that she was not only in a state of shock but was bitterly angry that he had died and left us—no, left *her!* She was deeply resentful of this final and irrevocable separation from her adored father. I was aware that only a part of her recognized that Bob and I were also suffering. She could not accept the raw hurt inside her—the hurt which left no room for sympathy with anyone else's pain.

When I had to tell the children that their father had cancer and did not have long to live, Myra had raged, "But he's only forty! Grandma and Grandpa are in their sixties and Aunt Tessie is over seventy. Daddy is too young to die!"

Forty does not really seem young to a teenager, but Myra resented the fact that other relatives were older and still enjoying good health. She would gladly have exchanged their longevity for a few more years with her father.

I understood so well all the torment the cancer was putting on our family, but most of all what it was doing to Myra.

Just as a young body has to build up immunities to disease, so does a young mind have to learn to accept heartbreak along with joys. But Myra's world had always been safe within our circle of family love and family sharing. Even heaven seemed within her grasp. We had always stressed God's love and she was secure in the certainty of His protection. We never had thought to make her aware that illness and death were part of life and must be expected and accepted in the same way we accept success and health. Perhaps we had overprotected Myra.

I gazed down at Paul, laid out in a full dress suit, which he had worn as first violinist and concertmaster of the City Symphony Orchestra where, as chief player representative, he was called upon to advise and keep technical business in order. His artistic hands were folded across his chest. I recalled how often our hands had been held lovingly in his.

He had taught Bob to play the piano and when Bob began to pick out notes of original songs, Paul showed him how to write a musical score. Today, Bob has melodies under copyright.

Paul had also taught Myra to play the violin. His fingers had helped her cradle the instrument under her chin and to bow melodies out of scratchy sounds. She loved the violin because she loved him. He and music were so inseparable that one had to love them equally. Paul found time to be my husband, companion and best friend. We had always looked directly into each other's eyes when we talked, using the secret sharing smiles of lovers.

Then cancer struck. The music faltered—and died.

Paul fought hard. He followed all the medical advice, all treatments. He went for an operation. The surgeon told us, "We have done everything medically possible. We cleaned out all the malignant cells we could find. Now it's in the hands of God."

How quickly the flesh had fallen from him. He had always stood so tall and dignified. He had been so strong. Suddenly he began to tire easily. He had to take prolonged rests. The spasms of pain seemed to last longer. He never complained, but when the pain came, he would withdraw from his favorite pursuits, from his work and from us, his family.

We clung together more closely, joking, laughing, making life as happy as we could, forcing away our fears and not looking directly into tomorrow.

I recall—and I will remember forever—the last time we saw Paul alive. Bob and I had been with the physicians and when we hurried to his room, we found Myra beside him, her hands in his. We heard him say, "It's going to be hard to say good-bye to you and Bob and Mother."

Almost in a frenzy, Myra begged, "Stay with us!"

"I'm too tired. I hadn't meant to drag this out. It's cost so much ... there's nothing left for you...."

A sudden paroxysm of pain gripped him. His breathing became labored. I flew down the corridor, frantically calling, "Nurse! Nurse!"

The nurse rushed in. One look and she raced to get help.

We were relegated to the waiting room. It only took twenty minutes. But when the doctor came out, we knew by his face. Paul was gone.

In the following days of mourning, people came to us, telling of Paul's sympathetic help, his tolerance, his understanding. One evening, with the company gone, I recalled the last thing Paul had said, "There's nothing left for you...."

Nothing left?

I repeated those words to Bob and Myra, then said, "Your father thought he had left nothing, but he left us everything to make us proud. He put music into our lives. I can go back to teaching music. Bob will compose and you, Myra, will go in your father's footsteps, bringing happiness to people through your violin playing. Everyone has to die, but daddy has given us much. His heritage lives beyond him!"

I saw that Bob was reassured by my words. But Myra remained secluded in her grief. During the night, I was drawn to her room, hearing the long, gasping sobs which she could not smother in her pillow. I sat down at the edge of her bed and took her in my arms.

She had cried so much that her words came out like hiccups. "Why did daddy die? I asked God to save him. God didn't. I hate God. He has daddy and I have nothing!"

"Hush," I soothed. "God gave us daddy so we could have everything. We have all the things daddy taught us. He left a musical testament through us, his family. In his time, Bob will do the same for his children and you will do the same for yours. In that way, daddy stays alive forever. Death is not the end. Just a different beginning."

She did not accept this. She was not emotionally ready for this final separation which seemed to have no reason.

Suddenly I saw a reason she could accept and I told her. She looked at me, unbelieving. I watched her mull over what I had just said. The stoniness of her face began to soften. Her eyes glowed—not from tears—but from heart's ease.

Her smile came slowly and a peal of relieved laugher burst from her throat.

"I love you, mommy," she said, "My best, best friend and I do love God. Now I know that even God needs daddy." She hugged me as tightly as I hugged her. We understood now why daddy died.

After all, didn't someone have to keep order in the orchestra of heaven?

MOUSE HOUSE

(Dedicated to her precious daughter, Judith, whose story this really is.)

Miss Mouse, as she was named in the days of her captivity, never even saw the longhaired gray cat, Nimbus, who watched, then pounced, dragged her from her grassy home in the backyard, through the dog door and into the spacious house.

Nimbus might have devoured Miss Mouse in a leisurely fashion, but the Mistress, ever on guard, was ready with a jet water gun.

She sent the liquid out in a stream. The drenched cat, quite disgusted with the lack of human gratitude and appreciation, dropped her prey and headed toward the basement, which served as her sleeping place and sanctuary.

The Mistress, horrified at the plight of the trembling mouse, was prepared, through long experience with these unpleasantries. She had a twelve-inch square wire cage ready, into which she put Miss Mouse, lifting her by the tail and setting her inside. Then she put in a small cup of water, some cheese and shredded paper for bedding.

For several days, Miss Mouse lay in one spot, trembling. Eventually her fright diminished. She drank and ate and burrowed into her paper.

Mistress watched until the day she saw Miss Mouse start moving, first with a tentative dragging motion and then with a limping scamper. When the latter occurred, Mistress took the cage out to the driveway, facing the woods. She opened the door. Miss Mouse was in no hurry to trust an open door. The humans went away, watching from out of sight.

Out the door ventured Miss Mouse, whiskers quivering, face lifted. She smelled the air. She looked about. Nothing moved. No sound. No stir.

Finally, she scampered for the woods and disappeared. Whether she lived to the ripe old age of mousehood, or whether something else out there enjoyed dining with her, we will never know. Miss Mouse never returned. Mistress still watches the cat. But, thus far, there has been no other tenant for the wire cage. Mouse House is up for sale.

ON THE PLATFORM

The day was misted. It was eerie, standing alone on the usually congested railroad station. The train had just pulled away and Henry, realizing another train was not due for half an hour, set his briefcase down. Straightening up, he beheld a ghostly figure. What should he do? Should he bolt? Should he wait for other passengers to arrive? His quandary was settled when the figure began to move toward him.

Frozen, Henry stood there.

The figure, coming closer, turned out to be—not an apparition brought on by the distortion of mists—but a real person of flesh and blood. The Stranger carried a briefcase similar to the one Henry had set down. Without a "by your leave" he gave Henry his bag, took Henry's and went off, leaving the place with hurried strides. Soon he was gone and Henry was once again on the platform, alone.

Not comprehending any of this, Henry decided to investigate the briefcase the other had left. Opening the case, he was amazed to see bills stacked in denominations of one-hundred dollars. He could not even imagine how much money was there. He closed the case.

Henry turned and began to walk swiftly off, deciding not to wait for his usual train to get him to work. He thought he had a good deal. Whatever reason the Stranger had for leaving him wealthy, Henry was grateful for the exchange of money for the lunch, pajamas and underwear packed by his wife for the business trip he wouldn't need to take ever again.

PARENTS' GROWING-UP PAINS

When my daughter went on her first date, I promised myself I wouldn't panic. She was out with a boy I did not know and, as the hours dragged toward midnight my stomach began churning.

"Come to bed," my husband advised. "Meg will be all right." I realized his optimism was for my sake. He was as uneasy as I.

"I'll read a little longer." I said. He went to bed and I turned pages I did not even see. I don't know how I survived until half past twelve when I heard Meg's key turn in the lock. Standing just outside the door she said goodnight to her date, her voice so light and gay that relief filled me.

I did not want her to catch me waiting up so I crept into bed quickly. My husband inquired softly, "Is she home?" He too, had been unable to sleep.

"Yes, but shhh! Pretend to be asleep." A light flashed on in the foyer. Meg came to our door, but when she did not move on, I realized she wanted to talk to us. I lifted my head, "That you, darling?" My husband switched on the light. "Want to tell us about your evening, Princess?"

In a flash, she plunked down on the bed beside us. Eyes shining with the radiance of a first romance, Meg recounted her lovely evening. "… He invited me out again next Saturday night.…"

I thought of the long, dreadful evening we had just undergone. I foresaw an endless repetition of such nights.

"Darling," I said, "It is beautiful that you are so happy, but we must confess that your father and I were worried about you all evening."

She was incredulous. "Worried? Why? You knew I was only going to the movies." It was hard to mar our child's Cinderella-at-the-ball feeling, but we knew this was the start of a new phase and guidelines had to be set down. "We knew the movie ended at eleven. You said you'd be home by twelve."

"Oh, mom, you just can't come right home after a show. We went for sodas and just talked. Anyway," she said defensively, "I didn't get home that much later—maybe forty minutes or so."

Her father gently explained, "When you expect someone at a certain time every minute longer seems out of proportion." Her expression said she simply could not believe that her doting parents were admonishing her after one of the most important events of her life.

"Meg," I put in quickly, "We are pleased that you are starting on a happy social life, but we must honestly tell you how this affects us. We want you to go out with friends and have dates, but because we love you so dearly we can't bear the thought of harm coming to you."

She was stupefied. "Harm! What harm?" I said, "There are a lot of crazies in the world. Parents just can't help worrying. We might feel better if you would phone us if you expect to be delayed."

"Others don't do that! It's babyish!"

"How can consideration be babyish? Perhaps it might start your friends thinking and doing the same things. Their parents must feel as we do, but maybe aren't as frank with their children."

My husband added, "Everyone talks about the generation gap. We haven't ever felt that and wouldn't want to start now."

"What your father is saying is that we don't intend to pry. We aren't that old ourselves that we don't remember times we told secrets to friends and not to our families. That's normal. But the same way that youngsters need to unburden their problems, so does our generation feel the need to tell our children if things bother us where they are involved. It isn't a big deal to make a telephone call that would alleviate our concerns."

Our daughter looked at us searchingly. Then she laughed and reached out her hands to take ours, "No, you crazy, wonderful people. It isn't hard. And I must confess it might make me feel silly at first to tell my date I have to call home, but it also makes me feel secure—knowing you are there, at the other end of the line—caring." She hugged us.

Frankness had drawn us closer. Growing up is hard—both on children and on parents. But growing up, with give and take on both sides—and with love—lessens the growing pains.

SENSES TAKING

On the television screen the glamour girl lays her head languidly back, half closes her eyes and with moist lips parted sensuously, places a dab of cologne at her throat and behind each ear. Almost as an afterthought, she dots each wrist.

Her ruggedly handsome date comes to the door. He does not say a word, just stands a moment—breathing—and his expression becomes one of instant passionate enslavement.

If that dab is good enough, I concluded, then how much more effective would a spritz be? If one spritz at throat, ears and wrists is good, two must be splendid. Spritzing, I go through each room of the apartment, until my date is finally at the door.

Encouraged by the way his eyes widen as I open the door, I explain: "Oh, you like my perfume?"

"Your perfume? I was looking for the flowers. I thought someone had died."

Small things like too much perfume can kill a romance. Of course, small things like garlic on the herb salad dressing can do the same. I recall once eating an onion pita for lunch, not aware it still lingered by evening. I found out it lingered when my date did not.

Do you remember the scene from Never On Sunday when our heroine wakes up, swishes some water in her mouth and is fresh for kissing at once? A swish of water could never vanquish the Bermuda onion on last night's hamburger. If I swished enough to achieve instant kissability, the environmentalists would "seek and destroy" for causing lower levels in the aqueducts.

Mouthwash commercials deride "medicine mouth." I would not take it unkindly if there was a pause between kisses and my guy asked, "Are you going for root canal work?" That is better than his never showing up again because of Gowanus Canal work.

How often have I cupped my hand over my mouth, hoping my nose would tell me if I offend. It tells me nothing. What tells is the fellow who leaves, saying his pet horse has colic, which leaves me wondering why Chanel #1 runs second to Stable #1.

I carried Binac in my purse for months. One spray could give me minty confidence.

When did I discover the vial was empty? When the lunch deli served garlic pickles with the knockwurst platter and, at my dinner appointment that evening, the antipasto at that Italian restaurant had salami with pungent cheeses.

It is hateful to be on the singles scene and be addicted to savory, spicy foods garnished, not with dill, but with leek. Once I asked an escort if he would try to give up smoking not because the tobacco odor was offensive on him, but because it clung to me.

"Sure," he said cheerfully, "Soon as you stop bubble-bathing. Fragrances give me hives." I had never suspected odors could cause reactions the same way that smoking did. Flowers cause allergies. Cosmetics cause rash. Offensive smells make you a loner.

You are left with a list of prohibitions. Don't eat the foods you love. Don't conceal your real face behind make-up. Don't date smokers. Don't use perfumes.

Bear all the above in mind when preparing for a date. It may not lead you to the altar. But it will definitely make you take leave of your senses.

SHADOW LOVER
(This is the story of a woman whose lover is an alien life form)

Jennifer pulled into her space in the underground apartment building parking area. Getting out of her car, she reached into her purse for her house keys and hurried toward the elevator. A sound behind her made her glance about. No one was there. Giving it no further thought, she pressed the "up" button and waited. Again a sound. She looked around. Nothing.

She could hear the elevator come to a stop at the parking level. As the door opened she felt a cool breeze brush past on her right. A vapor floated in. Had it begun to rain outside? What else could have caused the gust of mistiness?

She entered the car, pushed '4' and watched the closing door, then gazed at the floor indicators—'2', '3', '4'....

The door opened. She walked into the hall and down the corridor to '412'. She could feel the coolness at the nape of her neck. How odd.

Opening her door, she was ecstatically greeted by her small gray poodle Pan and his less demonstrative companion, her calico cat Tinker. Dropping her purse and keys on the hall table, Jennifer knelt and gathered up Pan, hugging him as he licked her face with frantic delight. Tinker purred and rubbed against Jennifer's leg.

Jennifer put the dog down and went to her phone to hear messages. There was one from her boyfriend, Todd Mueller. He was a biology teacher in Garrett High School. He was reminding her that this was Open School Week and he would be unable to see her for the next three days due to evening parent conferences. Jennifer had not forgotten, but felt a pang, missing her fiancée.

They had been a 'steady' since their high school days. They had a joint bank account and each contributed from his or her weekly salary, planning to be married when they could make a down payment on their own home. Jennifer would continue working until she became pregnant. Then she would leave her job as secretary to the legal firm of tax lawyers in the spacious office suite above the fashionable RAINBOW SHOP on Main Street.

The second message was from her mother: "Nothing new; just calling to say, 'Hi, Baby, I love you.'" Jennifer and her mother had a close and loving relationship. Although Jennifer still lived in the small Maine town where she had been born and raised, Mary, her widowed mother, had remarried. Her husband Carlton managed property in Los Angeles, so they had relocated to California. But mother and daughter phoned each other weekly.

Faithful to routines, Jennifer took care of her animals' needs. She cleaned the litter box, putting soiled articles into a paper bag. Then she scooped up Pan's newspaper wastes. He was paper-trained. She laid fresh newsprint out for him. Into the cat dish she put the contents of a can of food, plus some dry pellets. Into another dish went kitty treats. For Pan she opened moist dog food and added dry, along with treats and a few rawhides for him to gnaw at his leisure. She could hardly wait to strip out of her working clothes, take a leisurely shower and don a terry robe.

Her own supper was a Weight Watchers tray of food which she microwaved and ate at the kitchen table with some skim milk, an apple and 2 graham crackers. She nibbled some raisins while watching her evening TV shows. By ll:00 p.m. she was ready for bed. She opened her bedroom window from the bottom, enjoying the fresh air that ruffled her sheer curtains. She crawled under her sateen comforter and Pan leapt up, as usual, to sleep at her side, while Tinker took her place at the foot of the coverlets.

Setting her alarm for 6:30 a.m., Jennifer pulled the covers up to her neck and closed her eyes.

A cool, moist sensation on her face made her bring the covers up to wipe her skin. She may have fallen asleep, but a throaty growl from Pan roused her. She reached out a hand, found the dog shaking and backing away from her touch. He whined. At the same time Tinker uttered a yowl, leapt off the bed and fled the room.

Perplexed, Jennifer snapped on the light. "Pan! What is it? What's the matter?" The dog was on his belly, teeth bared and his eyes showing fear. Then with a yelp he jumped down on the floor and fled out of the room, after the cat.

Frowning, Jennifer looked about. She could see nothing that would send her pets into such a panic. But the glow of the light glistened on a spread of misty vapor, hovering over her. Unable to understand what was causing the gray moisture, she was about to sit upright when the muzzle came down upon her.

IT was light, much like the feel of fog during rainy, steamy weathers. IT lay upon her, almost without weight and even as she tried to guess what was causing the phenomena, IT sank slowly, gently, down upon her and into her body. IT immersed itself in her. It reached every part of her being. Invasion was her first thought. But, not violation! IT was taking her. IT was making her partner to a sensuous union. There was understanding of her every need and IT stayed in responsive sensitivity with palpable tactility.

Unending! Nor did she seek it to end—never having experienced such heights;

IT fulfilled her. IT made her quiver, glow. Desires were met and magically transcended, leaving peaked satisfactions that receded, only to swell again, to the very apex of arousal. Dawn came. IT left her. IT floated up and away through the partially opened window.

Jennifer gave a great sigh. She stretched and yawned and touched the stop button of her clock so the alarm would not go off. She felt as refreshed as though she had been in a deep sleep all through the night. What of the erotic dream? She thought ruefully and wondered if she dared tell Todd. Probably not. He would grin and say, "I'm coming right over. Just hold that mood!"

Her pets seemed their own selves again. Everything went its normal pace and, at the end of the day, after work, when she drove back to her garage space, she had designated yesterday as just a dream. Only when she left her car and headed for the elevator did she realize that yesterday's scenario was being repeated.

IT was back. IT rode up the elevator with her. IT came along down the hall to her apartment. IT entered along with her. Only this time, no dog or cat came to greet her.

With the feeling of wrongness descending upon her, she went into the kitchen, calling "*Pan! Tinker!*"

The two little pets were lying stretched out on the floor near their food dishes! A great fear gripped her heart. She bent to touch them. They were cold. She lifted each little limp figure onto her lap. They seemed to be asleep. But she stared, a numbness creeping over her. They were dead. There was no doubt. Still and cold. There was no response as she buried her face in their fur, her tears wetting them.

She did not know how long she stayed, bent over, holding her beloved furry creatures. All the time the mist stayed motionless. Finally she straightened up. Her heart was filled with fury. Her voice quivered with grief and anger.

"You did this!" she cried. "You killed them!" she raged. "Why? Why?" But she knew. The animals had been aware of IT. IT was threatened by their wish to protect their mistress. So, IT killed them.

She went to the phone. She dialed Todd's school. She asked that he be called to the phone. It took a long time because he was conferring with parents of his scholars. Finally, somewhat breathlessly, he was answering, "Jen, what's the matter?"

"Pan and Tinker are dead. I'll need you tonight. Can you come over after conferences?"

"Sure," he said, "It'll be a little late, but I'll be there. Go to sleep. I'll let myself in."

That should have comforted her. It didn't. She felt a foreboding. Had she made a mistake asking him here? IT was in the apartment. IT had already showed its power. Little memories of things she had read crept into her mind. Incubus! An evil spirit that descended upon and had intercourse with a sleeping woman!

Trying not to think, she wrapped each pet in its own little blanket. She took two tall garbage bags out of the box and put Pan into one and Tinker into the other. Fastening the bags with plastic ties, she carried them out of the apartment and downstairs to the outside hopper. She put the little bodies in and went back to her apartment.

IT was there. IT had not moved.

Not giving IT any attention, she went about her nightly chores while she waited for Todd to come. He never arrived. But the police arrived. They had found her address in his wallet when they went through his belongings at the hospital. Todd's car had skidded on the rainy streets and he had crashed into a lamppost. Todd was dead! Would she come to identify his body?

She went with the police. She made the identification. The police drove her home, asking if she wanted someone to stay with her that night. "No," she said, "someone is with me."

IT was in the kitchen where IT had been all the time. She stared at IT. She understood now what IT was doing. IT wanted her—only her. She knew IT was not through with its plan to isolate her, leaving only ITself in her life. She did not know who would be next. Perhaps, if she did not grow angry, or oppose IT, IT would take no further action.

She went to bed. IT came in all gentleness to enter with her in such a union as no woman had ever known.

When IT left in the morning, she stretched, much like a purring cat, almost narcotized against the traumatic events of the day before.

But reality was forcefully thrust upon her when she reported to work. Where the fashionable RAINBOW SHOP had been, with her firm's offices above, there was nothing but steaming wood from the fire hoses that poured water on the smoky demolished structure. An electrical fire in the night had destroyed it. Her job had gone up in flames. Her mind was in turmoil. The loss of her pets, of her fiancée, of her place of employment, was no mere coincidence. IT had done this—isolating her so there would be no one else in her life.

She went down the street, to the small coffee shop where she usually had lunch. They brought her the coffee she had ordered and, as she sat sipping it, her mind started to function somewhat.

Her job was gone. What would she do for money?

As though in answer came the remembrance of what Todd had done when they became engaged and had begun to plan for marriage. "I've taken out a million-dollar life policy," he had told her, the same night as he had slipped a diamond solitaire on her finger. "You're my sole beneficiary, Jen."

She had objected, guessing how expensive the premiums must be, but he would not be deterred, assuring her, "I'll be able to swing the payments. Don't forget I tutor outside my job and that money will go for the insurance. I love you, Honey and want you protected."

Now she would be protected. Todd's thoughtfulness had seen to that. She would be financially secure for life. Jennifer counted herself lucky. She had been a loved, protected person all her life. Her mother had always been there for her....

Her mother! Oh, Lord! She needed to call her folks!

Rushing to the telephone to call California, a terrible premonition assailed her. She almost fainted! Her folks were the only ones left in her life! If IT planned to isolate her then they were in terrible danger! The fright of that realization made the room grow dark! How could she possibly save them? What could she do to stop IT?

Excited voices from the patrons in the store drew her attention. The TV set was on. They were pointing to the screen. They were exclaiming in horror.

Another earthquake had hit California. Close to seven points on the Richter scale, it had wiped out the Alta Loma section, on the outskirts of Los Angeles!

Reeling, Jennifer caught the booth's door to keep from falling.

Her mother and stepfather lived in the Alta Loma district. Jennifer knew they were dead. Had IT brought on the earthquake? It was just too coincidental not to believe.

Now there was no one left in her life!

Almost as though her thoughts were directed, came a clear knowledge: She was her folks' sole heir! She drove home.

As always, IT was waiting for her at the elevator.

Up to her apartment they went together.

This time, when IT descended upon her, her mind was devoid of all other beings. Now she would give to IT all that IT gave to her—total possession ...

SMOTHER LOVE

"I'm killing my daughter?" Outraged and incredulous, I stared at my husband Bill across the breakfast table.

"C'mon now, Rena, I don't mean killing as in dead, but as in overprotective." Bill gave me an uncomfortable grin, gulped down the last of his coffee, planted a hasty kiss on my cheek and fled to his job. Bill hated unpleasantness and I knew he had brought up this touchy subject only because our eleven year old daughter Wendy had extracted his promise to speak up.

Only yesterday she had flared up at me, "I don't want you to come on this Girl Scout trip. The only reason you volunteered is because you want to keep an eye on me, not because we need more mother-helpers. You're just afraid to let me grow up."

"That's not true," I defended, but she began to list all of my actions she felt were out of proportion.

"You won't let me ride my bike to school because the roads may be dangerous. You won't let me go to the skating rink with my friends because I got pushed last year and needed stitches in my chin. That's an accident that probably will never happen again. And if I go to a Saturday afternoon movie with my friends you have to take us there and then you sit on the other side of the aisle so you can watch over me. When I go to a slumber party you make me telephone before we go to sleep and then you come to escort me home, even if it's only down the block. You're the only mother who comes to school with my rain things if the weather looks the least bit bad."

Wendy was right. But she was my only child and the fear that something might happen made me unduly cautious. I knew I should overcome my anxieties and give her more freedom. Perhaps next year, I would put it off as long as possible, because Wendy was still too young.

When it was Friday and we were getting ready to start the two-day camping trip, June Brown and her daughter May—Wendy's best friend—came to our house to pick us up.

We were crowded in the car, the four of us and our gear. June said that Ruth Dell had four girls in her car. And Terri, our leader, had her daughter and the balance of the supplies, in her compact.

Only seven of our troop would be there because the other two had come down with a stomach virus. I was secretly relieved that there would be fewer girls. We were pretty packed-in tightly now. When I had thought the others would be on the trip, I had told Wendy I would keep her on my lap, if necessary. She had stormed: "I'd rather stay home."

The drive was little more than an hour. We arrived at the campsite before five o'clock. Terri stopped at the council office to hand in the roster and the filled-in medical forms. They assigned us to our site.

There were three rustic lean-tos, with bunks built into the walls. It was definitely not my idea of ideal accommodations. I shuddered at the sight of the spider webs in the corner and the dead bugs the broom had missed. None of this bothered the girls, who were helping to unload the cars—each girl racing to claim possession of a bunk near her "best" friends.

Before Wendy could choose, I had her valise and mine on adjacent beds in one of the four-bed shelters.

"Put your things in the room with ours," I told May and Sandra Dill, who obediently did so.

Terri came over to say, "I thought we grown-ups would bunk together. Girls like to talk without adults around."

"Not Wendy," I answered quickly. "She knows I won't interfere with girl talk." At Terri's narrowed sidelong glance, I added hastily, "Besides, she tends to kick off covers while asleep and easily catches cold from drafts."

Terri seemed about to demur, but was called off to supervise placement of the food containers. The other four girls selected the cabin near us and Ruth, June and Terri settled into the remaining quarters.

Terri assigned some of the girls to work with two mothers over the grill, clearing away cold ashes and heaping on fresh charcoal. Others pumped clean water, to be used to prepare drinks and for washing. We had ice chests and canned soda, but for tonight, Terri preferred that the girls do as much of the preparations as possible.

Wendy and I worked, cutting lemons and squeezing them into the wide-mouthed jugs. As we worked, Wendy hissed at me, "I do not want you bunking with us. Go and sleep with the adults, like all the other mothers do."

I would not give in. She was close to tears and finally would not speak to me or anyone else. The franks and burgers we made on the open grills were smoky-tasty. Wendy did not touch any of the food—not even the marshmallows we toasted on sharp sticks. She only sipped the drinks and barely those.

When she got into bed, she drew the covers over her ears. Her pall communicated itself to the other two girls and they soon fell asleep. I did not know whether Wendy slept well or not, but I was uneasy in the silence of our room because I could hear the giggles from the other bunk, while ours was devoid of all girl-talk.

Then, it was morning. Terri woke us up. We washed and dressed. The girls and I tried to engage Wendy in conversation, but she was withdrawn and only answered in monosyllables, if at all.

During morning flag ceremonies, her mouth did not open for the pledge or national anthem and she stared stonily ahead. The entire camp had breakfast in the dining hall, then all walked to their individual campsites for the morning clean-up and inspection.

Arlene Pitt, a nature director, was introduced as our guide for the morning's ecology hike. She led us up the trail, stopping to inform us of the plants along the way. She showed us how to identify poison ivy and pointed out the animal tracks we might never have noticed. We all clustered around. But Wendy, listlessly, hung back.

"This is important," I tried to urge Wendy's participation. She did not even look at me. The road we traveled narrowed as we went further into the woods. At one point a small brook crossed the path and we had to step on slippery rocks to get to the other side.

I crossed gingerly, after the girls had nimbly skipped over the stones. I turned to offer Wendy a hand. She gave me a resentful look and moved further down the bank to get away from my outstretched arm.

As she was stepping on the first rock, I called, "Wait, Wendy, I'll help you." "Don't touch me," she gritted and missed the stone. Her foot plunged into the water. Instinctively, I rushed to help her get her footing, but she righted herself and was about to take the next stone, when she beheld me bearing down on her.

"Stay away!" she yelled, "I can do fine without you."

"I'll help you." I came on.

A strange expression crimsoned her face. She turned, looked over her shoulder, to where the woods encroached on the road. Before I realized it, she had dashed into the densest thicket. I gasped. "Wendy," I screamed. "Come back. You might get lost."

My scream got the attention of the others and they came scrambling back from the far bank of the stream to find out what was the matter.

"Wendy ran into the woods. Right there." I pointed toward some bushes which were still moving from her race through. I started to run to the spot where she had disappeared, but Terri caught my arm.

"Wait. If you go after her she'll go further in and might get lost. Just stay here. We'll call her." Terri hurried to the spot where Wendy had gone.

"Wendy," she called, "Please come out. You may lose your way if you go too deep into the forest."

We heard Wendy's voice. "Just don't follow me."

Arlene Pitt called to her. "We won't follow you. Just come toward the sound of our voices. Okay?"

"Is my mother there?" It seemed to me that Wendy's voice was not as near as just a minute before. Oh, God, she is moving in the wrong direction!

"Wendy," I screamed, "come back."

There was no answer. Arlene said, "Please don't speak to her, Rena. Let us try to urge her back."

"But she's my daughter," I was frantic. "She'll come to me."

Terri said, "That's the trouble. She won't come to you. She ran into the woods to get away from you."

Perhaps in other circumstances she might not have been that blunt, but she needed to administer this shock in order to silence me.

Arlene shouted, "Wendy, come toward the sound of my voice. Can you hear me?" There was no answer. I stared at Arlene with horror. She gave a small reassuring smile and cried out again in her loudest tone.

When there was no answer from Wendy, Arlene directed Ruth to go to the Council Office and get help. She had us all walk forward, keeping in close contact with each other. As we walked amid trees and brush, she called and directed us to urge Wendy to answer, but there was no response and we did not know whether Wendy was refusing to answer, or whether she had run further into the woods and could not hear us.

Under Arlene's guidance, we walked forward together, cajoling Wendy to talk to us. I was the only one who did not speak, realizing that it was my voice that had sent my child plunging deeper away. In my eagerness to protect her, I had endangered her very life.

In another half-hour, we heard more people join us. Arlene had us back slowly out of the woods, still fanning out, with finger tips touching. At the road there were Council officers and forest rangers. They told us they had sent word and people from the town would come to help in the search.

An hour passed. Then two. More and more people arrived. They followed the instructions of the rangers as to the search procedure so that they would not become lost in the area, too. They urged me to go back to the camp office to wait. Although I was reluctant to do so, I could not help remembering that it was the sight of me that had sent Wendy into the underbrush. I feared that if she heard my voice she would retreat deeper and deeper until there would be no hope of finding her. That thought so frightened me that I allowed myself to be led back and sat in a chair in the office, trying not to even speculate on the dangers Wendy might be facing from animals, or pitfalls of the region.

It was three hours before they found her. I thought a lifetime had passed. Her clothes were torn from the thorns, which had lacerated her skin. Her face was grass-stained and sooty. But she was the most beautiful sight in the world as she limped into the room where I waited.

The urge to run forward and gather her in my arms and touch her injuries to see how bad they were, was so strong that I had to hold the chair arms to keep from rushing to her. I had learned such a drastic lesson that I was more worried now about showing my feelings to Wendy, than I had ever been in her lifetime.

A ranger stood on one side of her and Terri on the other. Behind her clustered her friends and the people who had come forth to help in the search. Those dear, wonderful, lovely people. How could I ever tell them of my gratitude? I couldn't. Just as I could not now go to take Wendy in my arms. I could only stand, staring at her across the room, not daring to move.

It was Wendy who came to me. "Mommy," she said, "I'm so sorry for what I did."

"Oh, Wendy; Oh, baby," I cried and then I stumbled forward. We met half-way and were in each others' arms. We both asked forgiveness of the other.

"I'm sorry I babied you," I apologized. "I deserved it," she countered. "I was the biggest baby for running off. So many people were upset. Most of all, you. I'm so sorry."

"No, no," I mumbled into her hair, wetting it with my tears, "It was my fault. I promise not to baby you ever again."

She moved back a little. Her face was wet from crying. "You'll have to baby me sometimes. That's what mothers are for."

Yes, I thought. Mothers. But not smothers.

SPEAK EASY IN BROOKLYN

Just because Sir Winston Churchill's mother was born in Brooklyn does not make the borough an English colony! As a matter of fact we Brooklynites hardly understand the King's English, while the British are not sure English is spoken in here.

Thomas Moore wrote in 1815:

> Oft in the stilly night,
> Ere Slumber's chain has bound me,
> Fond Memory brings the light
> Of other days around me....

More than one hundred years later it still holds true; we still carry memories of the time the Dodgers were the home team and our dialect was pure ... *Brooklynese.*

We didn't say, "I cat the bahl." We said, "I cawt the bawl."

We were more inclined to catch the ball when the Dodgers were our team, playing at Ebbett's Field. But the Dodgers are long gone to Los Angeles and are known as The Angels, while Ebbett's Field has gone to that Great-Ballpark-in-the-sky, buried under a housing development.

A large chunk of Brooklyn pride left with "Dem Bums." That was the era when "th" was pronounced as "d" in words like "dose, dese and dem."

"Boids" nested in the tree that grew in Brooklyn. "Erl was for frying and "moidah" was a crime.

Two people conversing would sound like this: "Djeet?" "Yeah, Dju?"

"Soya wanna jern me fa cawfee?" Translated, this means: "Did you eat?" "Yes. Did you?" "So, want to join me for coffee?" Another sample of conversation between Brooklynites: "Howzya brudda Oinist?" "Heez gonna git hitched in an udder munt." "Ya godabe kidin! Woozda goil?" "Moitl Smit." "Sheeza looka. Watcheeseein Oinist. Heeza dog."

"Wunz meatsanuda's perzon" Translation: "How is your brother Ernest?" "He is going to get married in another month." "You must be fooling. Who is the girl?" "Myrtle Smith." "She's good looking. What does she see in Ernest? He's ugly." "One's meat is another's poison."

The literal spelling is used only to make strangers aware of the pronunciation. To natives, such enunciation is natural and clearly understood. If you are raised with birds, each chirp has significance. If you are a born and bred New Yorker, you are part of the melting pot of language and culture, brought in by the varied nationalities that have settled here. The language in Brooklyn may not be true American, but the people are.

So, if they call out, "Whynchawatchwaiyagoin?" just consider it a concerned citizen's way of cautioning you to take care. If they say, "Pleezta meechya," the correct answer is "Likewise."

If someone asks, "Whatimezit?" you might answer, "Treeclock," or "Fyclock."

Science fiction writers tell us of the time when humans will colonize other planets. When introductions are made with other life forms, one might say, "I am from Mars." Another might say, "I am from Jupiter. One voice will loudly proclaim, "Om fum Booklyn, Noo Yawk." You can be sure that every alien will know the speaker comes from the third world out from the sun—the planet called Oit.

THE DEVIL WITH PROTOCOL

Satan paced his office, forked tail lashing. He raged to his first demon, "Belial, I just passed the boiling oil unit. Bundy was telling Dahmer, 'This place is out-dated. It sure could use our input.' Yesterday I invited the Marquis de Sade to watch the newest sadomasochistic children's video tapes. He saluted. He was filled with admiration for the world's progress.

Has mankind put us to shame? Since Creation we've been the hottest show in town. Have we become jaded?

"Chief, our ratings have dropped since TV and movies put sex and violence on prime time. We've got to upbeat our image, starting on top."

"Top? You mean me?" Sparks flew. The three-headed dog Cerberus growled. "What's the problem?"

"Incentive. Remember when Hitler arrived. I suggested we greet him as befits a major monster. On earth, when honor is bestowed, heads of state wear ceremonial garb.

"I don't wear clothes."

"You would only wear them to greet VIPS who made Hell on earth. Prepare a banquet...."

"No one eats here."

"It's a civilized custom—very 'in' to wear white tie and tails...."

"My tail's red."

"There should be a cummerbund and a sash of honor across your chest—white gloves, top hat...."

"How will I get a hat over my horns?"

"We'll cut slits."

"Gloves?" He flexed his claws.

"Your Majesty," when Belial used that formal title his boss knew he meant business. "You need to become attuned to new times. Fine clothes command respect...."

"I don't command respect?" the Devil bellowed.

"Times have changed. Style has become very important. There is a saying, 'Clothes make the man.' You need Montague Montcalm, to outfit you properly."

"Who in perdition is he?"

"He's not in perdition, yet. But he is the top designer of men's clothes. You need the best."

Montague Montcalm was taking afternoon tea in his library. Amid fire, brimstone and thunder, Satan and Belial appeared. Coughing and waving his linen napkin to clear the air, the peeved Montague adjusted his monocle. "My dear fellows, if you insist on coming through the floor, can you do so without that hellish din?"

Satan matched his disdain "A gentleman would invite us to sit down."

"By all means, sit. Will you have a spot of tea and some crumpets?"

"No, I don't eat. I am the Prince of Darkness and this is my chief demon Belial."

"I guessed as much. Your travel cloak looks as if it's been through hell. Might I suggest that a being of your royal status consider a custom made wardrobe?"

Measurement and selection of materials began. Fittings proceeded rapidly. Satan's impatience set his tail lashing. Montague bound it about Satan with a sash in order to pull on the pants. His tailors helped fasten back the starched shirtfront and adjust the white bow tie. The jacket slipped on smoothly. Guiding the horns through the slits in the brim was tricky. It tilted rakishly.

"Finished," Montague declared, "I, who cannot be outdone, have outdone myself."

Satan, contemplating his reflection, admitted he was devilishly handsome.

Back home, Belial cajoled "Let's have a dress rehearsal." Not too reluctantly, Satan was persuaded. Demons, imps and the damned watched as their leader and attendants paraded past.

Circling the Lake of Fire, a burst of incandescence blasted out, blowing Satan's hat askew. As it dangled over one horn, he tried to right it. Struggling, his tail flailed out of its binder, tearing the trousers, exposing his backside. Satan bellowed. His vocal chords distended and snapped the bowtie, which became enmeshed in the shirt studs.

Belial, reaching for the tie, got his claw stuck in the shirt. Pulling, he caused the front to spring free of its fastening, tattering the cummerbund.

There was deep silence in Hell. Then someone tittered. Soon, everyone was laughing. Satan was stunned. Laughter in Purgatory! *And he was the butt of the joke!*

Casting the garments off, Satan shrieked, "I'll never practice diplomacy or protocol again!" He punctuated it with the most terrible vow in Hell: "Bless me if I do!"

THE GIRL INSIDE

In the St. Jude Senior Care Home, Sister Terry Dalrimple, who was called Nurse Doll by most of her charges, picked up the tray of morning medications and said to the young priest, "Father Altoni, as long as you are spending your entire first day here, you will enjoy meeting some of our residents. Just follow me." She led the way down the hall. The first door she came to was #12.

Before they entered, she explained softly, "Roberta Wane just turned 90. She has been with us about 6 years; a most active lady, participating in card games, acting in our plays, singing loudest at our Mass. Two months ago she suffered a stroke which affected her left side. She is now beginning to get more use of the left arm and leg. There is a slight twist to that side of her face, but by the grace of God it has hardly affected her speech. You will find her spirits excellent." As she added, "A real lady," she knocked and opened the door to a hearty welcoming, "Come in."

The slender lady was sitting in the chair, looking down at the courtyard below, where the gardeners were setting in new bushes. She was dressed in a yellow Victorian robe that matched the room's soft lemon color. She swiveled to face them, showing coloring as pastel as the light fruitwood chair and matching dresser with its large mirror facing across from the bed.

Her cheeks were a natural pink and her skin so smooth and unwrinkled it was hard to believe her age. Her eyes, bright and blue, were as curious as a young girl's. Fingering the crucifix around her neck, she cocked her head to one side, her brow raised in questions as she regarded the new face accompanying Nurse Doll.

"You know Father Malone retired. This is our new Father Altoni," the Sister introduced.

The patient smiled. "Then we'll have to call him 'Father Also'."

That reminded Sister Terry that it had been Roberta who had named her Doll. She would have to advise the priest that his nickname Father 'Also' would probably stick, just as Dr. Werter was Dr. Worry and their always-obliging custodian, John Switzer, was John Sweeter.

"When I was young, our family always used other names for us—pet names, mostly," Roberta explained and then amended thoughtfully, "although my brother Phil was called the Pill."

Roberta had endless delightful anecdotes about her family, but her folks and brother and sister were all gone now. "I have the longevity," Roberta nodded sagely and when her voice seemed sad she immediately changed the mood by recounting a funny incident or a recently heard joke. As she dutifully swallowed the medicine given to her, she announced, "Bobby will be here this afternoon."

Sister Doll smiled, "That's lovely. That's the third time this week."

The old lady nodded, "Since Bobby turned eighteen and got her driver's license, she can get out here more often."

"That's lucky for her." Sister Doll was loyal to her charge. She pointed to the right of the dresser, where a small gold-framed picture showed a pretty, dark-haired girl sitting at the top step, just in front of double doors with arched panes of a brownstone building.

Involuntarily the Father exclaimed, "Oh, she drives to New Jersey from New York?" Proudly Roberta amended, "That's Prospect Heights in Brooklyn. We always lived in the Heights."

"I'll come back and get you ready for Bobby's visit after I dispense the medication," the Sister promised and out they went.

When it was visiting hours, Father Altoni stood in the lobby to greet the visitors and be introduced to them. At the end of visiting hours, he realized that no one had come to see Roberta. "The old lady must be so disappointed," he thought. "I'll go in to see her when this break is over."

He headed for Room #12. He was about to knock when he heard Roberta laughing. "Bobby, you didn't really sneak that stray dog into the basement and bed him down with water and scraps? I did that at your age. My folks were furious when they discovered after a month that I never got rid of her. But, what could they do? I even named her Stranger, but I should have called her *The Gal Who Came to Dinner* because she stayed with us for fourteen years and even Pill started to care for her."

The young priest had not meant to eavesdrop, so he began to glide off down the hall, just as Sister Doll came along.

"Oh, I'm so relieved," he confided. "Bobby must have forgotten to sign in and I thought Roberta would be terribly disappointed. But Bobby's in her room after all. Is Bobby her niece, or her granddaughter?"

Sister Doll gave him a strange look. "No," she said sadly. "Bobby is the name the family gave to Roberta. Bobby is the young self we all have inside us. See?"

She opened the door to Room #12 just enough for Father Altoni to see Roberta propped erect in bed, talking animatedly to her reflection in the dresser mirror.

THE HAND OF LOVE

The letter from my son's elementary school principal informed me that Jimmy had made the Intellectually Gifted class. His math and reading comprehension levels made him eligible to do two years' work in one year when he entered junior high in September.

But it was the personal postscript that the principal added, which brought tears of happiness to my eyes.

He had written: "Jimmy is the finest, most normal eleven-year old boy I have ever had the pleasure of knowing." His use of the word normal made my throat grow tight with thankfulness.

Since Jimmy's birth I feared that he might not grow up "normal." That dread began the moment my obstetrician entered my hospital room after delivery. I took one look at the doctor's somber face and my heart sank.

"My baby," I whispered. "Something is the matter with my baby, isn't it?"

He nodded and said without preliminaries, "He was born with a deformity of the left hand."

"Deformity?" I could only stare. And when he explained the full extent of Jimmy's handicap, I felt the room reel, almost fainting at the horror of the revelation.

"He has a congenital malformation of the left hand. From the wrist down the hand is smaller. The three middle fingers are missing, unformed. But there is a short thumb and short pinky and with these he will be able to grasp objects. With practice he can strengthen his holding abilities and become quite proficient, even excel."

I heard a small croak of a voice come out of me, "What else?"

"Nothing. He is perfect in every other way."

Of course I did not believe it until Jimmy was put into my arms in bed and I could throw off the blanket to examine every tiny bit of him. My heart filled with gratitude as I saw for myself that the doctor was right. Jimmy was perfectly formed—a beautiful boy, with a fuzz of blond hair and big blue eyes.

Between surging relief at this and a sob in my throat at the sight of the undeveloped hand, I kissed the small pink palm, vowing to do everything possible to keep Jimmy from feeling different, or rejected. As parents, we would assure him of his importance and make it our business never to permit ourselves to feel unhappy or ashamed. With my husband Eli at bedside, we studied our alert infant and made this vow together.

We found it hardest when family and friends became aware of the handicap. I had to control tears when encountering the whispered conversations, exchanged glances and sympathetic suggestions. "Plastic surgery," was most often advised. We had clung to the hope that plastic surgery might cure Jimmy. But all the qualified orthopedists who examined him reluctantly advised that plastic surgery would not help. There was no bone structure between the knuckles and the nail stubs of the three fingers were missing. "Of course," the specialists always assured, "as research progresses there may be ways to help your child. Just don't give up hope."

We never did. But time would pass while we waited for technical advancements. For that we could wait, but not for the physical, emotional and spiritual assurances to make our child grow in confidence and courage.

Our first step was to enfold him with love. That was the easiest part of all. Jimmy's bright eyes, full of curiosity about everything, seemed always ready for smiling. He was eager and loving. We were lucky that even the fretful times babies have were minimal. Rocking, kissing, holding, talking, we soothed him even in the dreadful teething period. He appeared endowed with natural fortitude, as though God was preparing him for the rough stretches that most babies did not need to face.

Early in those developmental years, we taught him grasping and later, catching soft objects, then—gradually—balls. He became so proficient, he was able to reach up and seize any thrown object and hold it securely. He became poised and assured. We knew that when he grew older he would be sought by teammates for games. And that was what happened—much later.

Eli and I learned together how to love, but not overprotect; how to guide but not stifle initiative. There were times Jimmy was frustrated. Tying shoelaces, buttoning buttons—the fine tasks were more difficult than the gross tasks and required infinite patience of us all.

How much easier it would be for us to have tied those laces than to insist he do it himself and watch his cheeks grow redder with exertion and stand silent when tears of frustration rolled down his cheeks. Inside, we cried for him; outwardly, we were calm and watchful and ready to snatch him up in a dance of joy when he finally mastered a task and looked up, with a lopsided grin and triumphant eyes.

He never heard how we prayed as he toiled. He never heard my crying alone. But I heard his and had to judge when to aid and when to remain off to one side, in quiet waiting.

How shall I tell you of the new levels of complications that growing older brought? How shall I tell you of the little friends asking innocently, "What's wrong with Jimmy's hand?"

Calmly I learned to say, "He was born that way." My voice was smooth, but my heart was twisted. Entering kindergarten was a big trial. A secretary suggested a special school for handicapped.

"He doesn't need it," I looked straight into her eyes. That was proven quickly when he was able to keep up with other children in all activities and excel in most. He learned to answer, "I was born this way," when curious questions were aimed at him.

Children accepted him for himself. They were much more adept at that than adults, but Jimmy learned to answer all questions without embarrassment or annoyance.

During parent-teacher conferences, Jimmy's teachers were full of praise for him. "He helps other children with buttons and pulling on boots. When a child's zipper is stuck we know we can come to Jimmy to get it unstuck."

When Jimmy was promoted from the primary to the middle grades and there were ball games at lunch-hour, he would come home quiet, or pale with anger. "They won't let me play. They say I have a funny hand."

I cleared my throat, where the inevitable sick sob was beginning and managed calmly to advise, "Then you'll just have to prove you can play ball better than they. Daddy and you have played together so much and now you're better than daddy."

Head tilted to one side, Jimmy studied me. "I'll show them tomorrow," he promised. And he did. Daring them to hit the ball to him, then catching it easily, showing how he could swing the bat and send the ball up and over, then score home-runs while his opponents were still searching for the ball. Friendships developed and blossomed. He was liked. He was respected. And by his family, he was loved and he loved back.

Now he is graduating from public school with honors. That does not mean we have stopped hoping for the day science will be able to rebuild a whole new hand for our son. But we have not remained still, waiting. We offer to other parents the lessons Jimmy's life taught us, enabling us to grow along with his growing-up. We gained an abiding faith in God's decision to endow us with a child whose single imperfection would challenge us to turn disability into greater ability.

In our need to live with a purpose we became strongly unified as a family, tempering love with discipline and routines and thankful to God for his infinite wisdom and love of us by making Jimmy a "special" child, in every sense of the word.

THE MISTLETOE

In the hallway outside her closed bedroom door Ginny heard her mother's hysterical exclamation to the doctor: "Oh, dear Lord, no! She is only thirteen! Too young to be paralyzed! Too young to die!"

The doctor's soft indistinguishable words followed and then their voices faded down the hall. Ginny turned her head on the pillow, eyes enormous, gazing at the window where a holly hung. In the oval she saw the snow still falling. It was because the snow had blocked the windshield of the car that the driver had not seen her step off the curb and now she was going to die.

There was a curious hurt in her throat at that knowledge, a poignant nostalgia for things she had known and might never know again: sleigh rides in crisp snow that reddened her cheeks; balloons and birthday parties. But, most of all, pirouetting on tippy-toe in her silver ballet slippers, her net and tulle tutu rustling as she twirled on the polished floor of the class where she took private dance lessons.

Miss Kane, her teacher, had often told Mother that Ginny was her star pupil and showed great potential as a dancer.

"She's highly motivated. Some of the other students consider dance practice a chore, but Ginny loves it and works hard to perfect her technique."

Mother agreed. "Ginny often says she will be a ballerina when she grows up."

Now Ginny grieved, "But not if I can't walk; and not if I'm going to die."

Strange, she did not feel like a dying person. Her head was so clear. She didn't even feel pain. The doctor had said that was because the accident had injured her spine. She did not feel pain—except in knowing she would not be able to walk—or dance again.

Anger started to throb and grow inside her. She felt cheated. Tonight was Christmas Eve. Also, it was her thirteenth birthday and they had planned to have a birthday-holiday party. She had even helped drape the tinsel over the tree in the living room. She had been so very careful, handing the fragile Christmas balls to her parents to hang on the boughs.

She had spent hours with her friends making up and discarding lists of boys to invite. The girls had had a club since they had been eleven; but this was to be the first co-ed party their parents sanctioned. Because they had not dated previously they'd had all the fun and all the arguments that went into a selection of ten boys from the their classes to invite.

"My mother says we can put up a sprig of mistletoe," Ginny confided. The girls were wide-eyed. None had ever been kissed by a boy and the mistletoe became the ultimate, the cherry atop the icing of delicious expectations. But not for Ginny now.

The doorknob turned. Mother came in quietly. White-faced, a brave smile trembling upon her mouth, she moved to the bedside, sat beside her daughter and lifted Ginny's fingers to her lips, kissing them one by one. She regarded the girl with the same forced, studied brightness. "Are you comfortable, dear? Do you want anything?"

Ginny nodded, "I want the party to be held tonight, Mother, just as we planned it." The hand holding hers shook. After a while her mother said, "Of course, darling. The party will go on as scheduled."

By evening the snow had stopped. With some difficulty Mother dressed Ginny as she requested, in the pretty tutu with the short skirt, gathered in a froth of net and tulle. It had been hard drawing the clothes over the bandages and braces and when it was done Ginny was exhausted, but she would not allow her mother to even consider a cancellation.

So the dainty, silver ballet slippers were slid on her feet and bound around with glossy, satin ribboning, appearing for all the world as though ready for music to start and the dance to begin—poor feet that would never walk or dance again.

Mother combed Ginny's hair and arranged it in lovely loose waves about her face. Then she applied make-up to Ginny's paling cheeks and lips. When the doorbell rang, announcing the first guests, Mother lovingly kissed Ginny's temple, assuring her she would be "right back and daddy will carry you downstairs." Then she left.

Lying there in the soft light of her twin dressing-table lamps, Ginny again felt that surge of anger at being cheated. It gave her strength If she was going to die anyway she would at least have this last wonderful time, at her own party, getting her first kiss under the mistletoe. That gave her the determination to fling back the covers. She willed herself to walk—and she did.

She walked across the room. When she came to the head of the stairs she could see Mother talking to new arrivals at the open door. The mistletoe hung from the lintel between the hall and the living room. A boy turned around and looked straight up to where Ginny stood at the top step.

"Hello," he smiled. Although he looked familiar, Ginny could not remember his name. Yet he was the handsomest boy she had ever seen. "Come down," he called and intentionally stepped beneath the mistletoe. Ginny had never felt so light before. In her silver-spangled skirt and satin ballet shoes she fairly floated down the stairs.

The boy clasped her hands. "Now there'll be no more pain and you'll walk and dance again."

Upstairs Ginny lay on the bed, with the happiest smile on lips that were growing cold. But downstairs, Ginny was under the mistletoe, breathless face raised for her Christmas birthday kiss, in the tender embrace of the boy whose name she just realized—Death.

THE SACRIFICE

Behind the Salter farmhouse the creek stones lay bare and dry and the tree branches hung limp and still. Ten-year old Kathlyn felt the heavy depression the August drought had brought upon the rolling hill country. Neighbors met in the Salter house to discuss the latest foreclosures brought about by a government that gave little support to farm credit. Their bitter voices frightened her and she wished she could close her hearing to the anger they vented against the credit associations who appropriated their machinery for auction.

The land on either side of the Salter property had been foreclosed and the families had moved away. To Kathlyn it meant a loss of friends and a loneliness that no other summer vacation had known. She counted the days until the Bookmobile turned off the main road into their drive. Shelves built into the van held books on all topics, but Kathlyn never deviated from the place in the corner where the fairy tales, myths and legends were kept.

"Haven't you read them all yet?" Miss Arlene, the book volunteer would invariably ask her.

"No." There were always those stories Kathlyn had not read, or those she wanted to reread. She borrowed the maximum number of books permitted. At home she made sure to get her chores done as efficiently and quickly as possible so there would be time to read. She read vociferously, finishing the books a day or two before the Bookmobile returned.

One disappointing Thursday the van failed to show up. Kathlyn did not know that Miss Arlene was sick and had asked the town librarian to telephone all her stopovers to say she would be there the following week.

When the Salters received the call, Kathlyn was not aware of it. She had already walked impatiently down the road, hoping to encounter the Bookmobile. She was walking and watching for the swirl of dust that would give advance notice of the approaching vehicle. Suddenly a different movement caught her eye.

She stopped. A girl was skipping down a wide, curving driveway, leading out to the road where Kathlyn stood. When the girl reached her, Kathlyn's breath caught in her throat. She had never seen anyone so beautiful. A dainty girl of Kathlyn's own age, the stranger had great blue eyes and waist-length hair as fair as silver, caught up by a satin, silver ribbon.

It was not Sunday, but her short flounce of a dress had a spotless white pinafore that made Kathlyn aware of her own faded washed-out denims. But the other's friendly smile put her at immediate ease.

"My name is Mia. I live up there." She waved toward the big white house on the hill summit.

"I'm Kathlyn. My folks have the farm down the road. Are you new here?"

"Not really. Father's president of the bank in Moore." That was the city bordering the town. "All year round I go to private schools and we spend our summers at resorts, but Mother's sister Lynn is sick, so this season Mother goes with Father when he drives to work. She stays with Aunt Lynn and I stay here with Nana. When I saw you coming along I thought it would be nice if we could be friends. This is a lonely summer. We have a glider swing in that bunch of trees. Wouldn't you like to sit there and we can play together?"

"Oh, yes, but I have to tell Ma. She worries if she doesn't know where I am."

"I'll wait," Mia promised.

In spite of the heat, Kathlyn ran the quarter mile back home. In the living room the meeting was still going on. In the kitchen her mother was wiping down the droplets of condensation from the cans of cold beer and soda. Everyone chipped in for the drinks when they held their meetings.

"Ma," Kathlyn cried, "there's a new girl on the second hill going east toward town. Her name is Mia. Her folks are very rich, but they can't go away this summer. Can I play with her?"

Her mother turned with the sodden towel in her hand and looked hard at Kathlyn, but the girl realized that her mother was not really concentrating—being more attuned to the discussions taking place in their living room. Kathlyn took her silence for consent and hurried off, calling back over her shoulder that she would return before sundown. As she hastened to her new friend she was thinking, "Mia calls her folks Mother and Father. I call mine Ma and Pa."

It was when she met Mia's parents, some days later, that Kathlyn realized they could not be addressed otherwise. They were spare and erect. He wore a white linen suit, jacket and tie, even in this heat. She wore light chiffon and white lace gloves. They did not disapprove of their daughter's new friend. Their cool acceptance was part of their reserved upbringing, but their distant eyes warmed to their daughter and both of them kissed and held her tightly before they drove off in their limousine.

Mia spoke to Kathlyn of the warm lands in the south of France and in Spain. The Mediterranean Sea was as casual a swimming area to Mia as the creek was to Kathlyn.

Kathlyn told Mia of the problems of the drought. Although Mia was far from such troubles she was sympathetic. She had a wonderful imagination and had read as widely as Kathlyn.

"Do you remember the story of the Indians who needed rain and did a dance to their gods? We could try that."

The two girls made up steps that seemed appropriate. After some practice they danced in unison, heel-toe, a bend forward, straighten up, a bend back. For half an hour they danced under the cool shade of the grove trees. They let out soft whoops as they had seen Indian dancers do on the TV screen. Loud sounds might have drawn the servants from the house.

They did their rain dance every day, but the rains still did not come. It was in the third week of their meeting that Kathlyn told Mia she had thought of a way to bring on the rain. She had read many legends of many peoples. Hawaiian folklore told of the sacrifice of a selfless maiden who threw herself into a volcano to bring rain to her parched nation. In African tales youths flung themselves from high peaks. Indians gave up their living hearts to the priest's knife.

Kathlyn was practical. There were no volcanoes and no high peaks. But there were knives. Mia turned pale. "No. No. You must not even think of doing that."

Kathlyn wavered. It was certainly the ultimate sacrifice. She must really give more thought to such a drastic deed. But when she returned home, her mother was standing at the back door, staring at the dying crops.

"Oh, God," she whispered. "why doesn't it rain?" Ma was crying, so Kathlyn knew she must do something soon. The knives were always sharp. Pa whetted them, like a ritual, against a stone outside. Kathlyn chose a thin blade, one of several table knives used for cutting meats. She wrapped it in paper toweling and put it into her school tote. Going out, she called, "Ma, I'm going to play with Mia. Be back before supper."

Before supper, she hoped the rain would fall. She had prayed very hard all night. She had promised God the sacrifice if He would cause the rain to fall.

Mia was sitting on the glider, but there was no usual smile on her face. She knew what her friend meant to do and she did not know how to stop it. She told Kathlyn how much she had agonized during the night and the two stared at each other, eyes glistening with tears.

"I heard them say there might be a chance for showers soon," Mia offered hopefully.

"It was on this morning's news."

Both girls looked up at the pitiless blue sky that showed barely wisps of white clouds. Not a single rain cloud to be seen. Still Mia tried to dissuade Kathlyn. "Let's try our rain dance. This time let's pray a whole lot, too."

Kathlyn laid aside her tote and stood shoulder to shoulder with her friend. They began to dance slowly. In her head Kathlyn heard her prayer: *"Make it rain. Dear God, please make it rain."*

The words ran through her mind like a tumbling torrent and finally spilled out to her lips, pleading at first, then fiercely—in an agony of desire. Rain. *Rain!* Let it start today. Let it save the crops. Let it save our farm. Let it save the people, the animals. Rain! Rain! RAIN!

Dancing, dancing, chanting, chanting, "Rain. Rain ..." they finally fell together on the soft, moist grass and lay there, utterly exhausted. They fell asleep, arms about each other. It was almost dusk when they woke. They could not distinguish the overcast of sunset from a sky that might possibly hold rain. Kathlyn feared she had no alternative but to do the sacrifice.

Mia rose, dusting loose grass from her skirt. She looked at the menacing tote Kathlyn picked up. Alarm came into her voice: "Let's wait one more day! Maybe tomorrow...."

Kathlyn shook her head. "Ma's crying all the time when Pa's not around to see. Pa can't get all the chores done because he has to go to the town hall and march and carry signs. He's so tired when he comes home and hits the table with his fist. He says politicians won't consider little farmers. Then he and Ma come into each other's arms and she says, "What are we going to do?"

Kathlyn gazed down the slope at the lawn of Mia's property where the grass was always green, the trees gave shade and drought was not a concern. Mia had told her they had an artesian well and irrigation ditches. Rich people could afford those, but Kathlyn's folks were dependent on the weather. So Kathlyn knew what she must do. Another day would not matter. They had danced for rain. They had prayed for rain. Now they must make the ultimate sacrifice for rain.

Kathlyn took the knife out of the tote. She unwrapped it, stuffing the paper back into the bag. When she held up the blade, it shone silver. Silver seemed right for the hair that hung soft to Mia's waist. Silver seemed right to match the shine of the tears in Mia's eyes.

"Oh, Kathlyn, you are the dearest friend I ever had. I shall miss you so much. I shall be so lonely. There will be nothing without you."

Kathlyn's eyes were also wet. She was not sure—not even now—that she could take life, but she steeled herself with the reminder that a sacrifice would end the drought. She was certain of that. All the legends told that prayers alone could not be effective. There had to be a sacrifice.

With a resolution she did not know she possessed, she lifted the knife. Mia sadly took the silver ribbon out of her hair. She held one end, extending the other into Kathlyn's hand. They clasped the silk, taut between them.

Kathlyn looked one last time into the brimming blue gaze of her friend, then holding the knife high, brought it down with a swift stroke. The ribbon was cut in half and fluttered like a dying leaf, to fall limp and motionless between them.

Mia sobbed, "I'll miss you. I'll be so lonely. Will you remember me?" Her voice was fading.

"Always. Always!" Kathlyn whispered.

The heat was shimmering all about. It seemed so intense that the pink frock of Mia vaporized as her soft skin wavered into ghostlike paleness.

The last thing Kathlyn saw was the silver luster of Mia's gaze, beseeching and then fading. Kathlyn was alone in a grove where trees hung, listless. The grass was brown. The glider was gone. As Kathlyn raised her tear-filled eyes to the crest of the hill, the big white pillars of the house receded in fog and then the house itself wavered to vapor and disappeared.

Slowly Kathlyn rewrapped the knife and put it back into the tote. She moved down the old dirt road that had not been used for more years than she knew. With bent head she walked home.

She was near the back porch when she felt the first small droplets. She lifted her head, stared up at the sky that was darkening with clouds, scudding in a swift wind. She held her breath, unable to believe that rain was actually falling. With drops spattering her chin, she took the steps in a leap, flung open the back door where Ma and Pa sat at the kitchen table.

"It's raining!" she cried. They leapt up. They raced outside where the moisture hit their faces. Then they hugged each other and danced about like children, saying, "It's raining! It's RAINING!"

They held their hands out to take Kathlyn into their dance, but she shook her head.

"I had to sacrifice to make it rain. Mia's gone."

Pa looked mystified, not understanding what she meant. Sadly, Ma explained, "Out of loneliness, Kathlyn created an imaginary friend. She gave Mia up for our sake." She gave a sad sigh. "Our daughter is growing up."

All the wistful regret was in Ma's voice because she understood that Kathlyn had put an end to a cherished dream. Ma knew there would be no return to childhood for her little girl ever again.

WOMEN, WOMEN, EVERYWHERE

The taxi stopped in front of the Hotel Marlowe. Out stepped an attractive gray-haired woman in her late sixties. Those seated on the porch ceased their conversations, leaning forward to survey the newcomer. One of the women, wrinkled and buxom and wearing a platinum wig, said to the elderly lady next to her, "Here comes a new one."

"What?" the other shouted, adjusting her hearing aid, "What did you say?"

"I said here comes a new one."

"Oh!"

Irene Harper dug into her pocketbook to pay the driver of the taxi. "Please take the bags into the lobby," she said, as she viewed the ladies with a sinking heart.

The last time she and her husband Joe were in Florida, they had passed a hotel just like this one and she had said, holding on to his arm possessively, "Women, women, everywhere. And most of them widows. I'm so glad I'm not one of them."

Now she was a widow of six months, trying hard to adjust. She went inside the hotel. There were old people seated in the small lobby; some dozing, others watching the color TV. At the far end of the room, others were playing cards in an adjoining room.

Her room was small and dark. The windows looked across a narrow alleyway to the blank brick wall of the hotel opposite. In her room there was a bed, a sink, a stove and cabinets. The cabinets contained an assortment of dishes, pots and one frying pan. It reminded her of those lingering Sunday morning breakfasts Joe and she had always enjoyed so much.

Her throat felt tight. Joe was gone and so was the home they had shared for 40 years. She had watched tearfully as their beloved possessions were loaded into a moving van, to be placed in storage until she could decide what to do with them. A heart attack of her own had precipitated this move to Florida.

So here she was! Irene swallowed hard. The climate might help her heart, she thought ruefully, but she could very well die of grief and loneliness. There was a timid knock on her door. "Yes?" She opened the door an inch and peered out. A pleasant blond woman smiled at her.

"I'm Betty Hirsh, your next door neighbor," she said, "Welcome. Do you play cards?"

"Why yes," Irene replied, "I do. But I haven't played for some time."

"That doesn't matter. It's like driving a car. It will come back to you. I'll let you know when we need a hand. See you later," and she went off.

Irene smiled, remembering a friend saying. "If you play cards, you won't be lonely in Florida."

Perhaps this was true. And it might help, but could she overcome the loneliness of night with its memories of Joe? Sleep was restless that night, so she rose early and dressed. She went to a corner restaurant for breakfast. After that she stopped at a 7-11 store and purchased food to keep in the small refrigerator the hotel provided. She rested awhile, wrote letters and then went down to the hotel lobby. As she was getting out of the elevator, a plump attractive woman about her own age stopped her.

"I'm Lily Barth. I heard you just checked in. A widow?" Irene nodded.

"Listen, don't mope around with this rocking chair brigade. There's social dancing tonight at the park. Walk over with me! The admission is only 25 cents."

Irene knew the place. She had been there many times with Joe.

"Oh no," she protested. "It's only six months since my husband died. I can't go dancing. Not yet, anyway. It's too soon."

Lily Barth gestured with both hands in mock despair.

"My dear," she said, "I felt the same way when I first came. You don't have to dance if you don't want to. Just watch."

Lily was right. Anything was better than sitting around. Irene decided to go with her. She promised herself to try to make a new life. She fussed that evening getting dressed; applying a dab of rouge to her pale cheeks and choosing one of the new outfits her daughter insisted she buy before she left for Florida. It was a pink linen suit. Pink—Joe's favorite color.

Tears blurred her eyes as she started to brush her dark hair, streaked more plentifully with grey since Joe's death. There were more wrinkles too, nesting near the corners of deep blue eyes. She was ready when Lily knocked on her door and called "All set?"

"Yes." Irene joined her. It was a beautiful night. A full moon sailed over Miami and the cloudless sky was filled with a huge amount of glittering stars.

Irene was in control until Lily and she reached that same municipal park where Joe and she had so often sat on the hard wooden benches listening to the music. That same music was now playing.

I can't go in, Irene thought miserably. Why did I let Lily talk me into this?

Lily asked, "Got your quarter?" Irene nodded, following Lily in because she simply did not know how to back out. It was Saturday night and people were already dancing. They found an empty bench and sat down. A man that Lily knew walked over.

"I was looking for you," he said, "Care to dance?"

Lily turned to Irene. "Do you mind?"

"No, of course not."

Irene glanced around. Nothing had changed since she was here with Joe. The dancers were the same with different faces; some of them were elderly widowers who hadn't danced in years and now, having taken lessons, let loose like teen-agers. Some were married men who came without their wives. And there were those who came with the hope of meeting someone to date.

The orchestra played a soft piece and even before the singer began to sing, Irene recognized the tune. It was 'Because Of You', the song Joe and she had always referred to as their song. It had been sung to them at their wedding. Irene's eyes became bright with tears.

She started, as a man's voice said gently, "Please don't cry. Can I help?" She looked at the man. He was of average height, a little heavy, but sun bronzed and nice looking with a thick mop of silver hair. His voice was sympathetic.

By now the tears were rolling down her cheeks. He handed her his handkerchief. She dried her eyes. The music ended. It helped her to gain control.

"Feel better?" he asked.

"Yes. Thank you." She returned his handkerchief and because she felt she needed to explain, she choked out, "My husband Joe died six months ago."

"I'm so sorry;" he meant it truly. "I know how hard it has been for you. I lost my wife last year and still can't get used to my loss. But it's important for people to keep from getting lonely. My name is Ben Zimber."

"Mine is Irene Harper." He was easy to talk to and gradually the hurt lessened. They were unaware the music had ended until Lily returned explaining that her escort had invited her to Shanley's. "That's the cafeteria where everyone goes for coffee," she explained.

Irene made the necessary introductions, then said, "I know Shanley's. You two go, by all means. It's all right."

"Well, you can't walk home alone," Lily said, giving Ben an oblique glance. The man next to Irene spoke up quickly. "I will see the lady home if she will allow me." Lily threw him a grateful glance. "That's fine," she said and went off with her escort.

Ben said, "Perhaps we could go for coffee, too."

"You're very kind," Irene said, "but I'm not dating yet. It's too soon. Please understand." The sadness had crept back into her voice. He pressed her hand gently. "I understand."

They walked home in pleasant silence and she was beginning to feel more at ease with Ben when the wail of an ambulance pierced the quiet night. As Irene watched, the flashing red lights of the emergency vehicle ripped past them and disappeared in the direction of Miami Hospital. She was reminded of the time she had accompanied Joe in an ambulance just like it.

She began to tremble violently and a cold chill gripped her heart. What was she doing here, with this stranger? Who was he? She had been holding on to his arm. Now suddenly, she let go. They walked in silence.

As soon as they reached her hotel, Irene stopped on the street directly in front and said quickly, "Thank you. It was nice meeting you. Goodnight!" She ran up the steps. He called after her, "I'll phone. I know your name and your hotel."

He called her several times after that and his persistence was beginning to wear her down. But then there would be some little thing, another reminder of Joe and the pain would begin all over again.

"It's no use," she thought. "There can never be another Joe."

She continued to refuse Ben's invitations until he finally stopped calling. "If you change your mind, you call me," he said. He gave her his phone number.

Several times after that, they met by chance in Shanley's Cafeteria where most of the seasonal visitors took their meals. He was always pleasant. And although he brought his tray over to her table and joined her, he did not repeat his request for a date.

After that, Irene spent her time walking and reading, even joining one of the senior citizen clubs where they gave interesting lectures and taught various card games. Somehow, the time passed.

Then the season was almost over. When Irene came into the lobby one morning, there was an announcement on the bulletin board that anyone interested in either remaining or renewing a room for the following season should see the manager.

"Are you staying on?" a voice behind her said. It was talkative Ellen Hayes who occupied room 212.

"I'm not sure," Irene murmured softly. But even as she spoke, she knew she would. It was this flood of feeling that made Irene pause. For the first time since Joe's death, she was able to experience a real emotion and this led her to think clearly. She realized she liked Ben—very much.

Ben would wait, he had told her. But next season was a long way off. And there were women, women, everywhere.

She took a deep breath; she flipped open her address book and dialed Ben's number. When he answered, she said softly, "Hello. This is Irene. Do we still have a date?" His quick, eager reply told her all she needed to know. "Of course. Let's make it for dinner—tonight."

NIBBLE, NIBBLE

Our annual family apple-picking was in full swing. My brother Hal helped fill my basket. "C'mon, Gert," he commanded. Because he was thirteen and I ten, I followed, as always.

Moving and picking, we found ourselves in a clearing with a tiny cottage. A smell of baking drew us to the door, opened by an old woman, inviting us, "Come inside for milk and cookies."

Hal pulled me away from the house, running. The delicious baking smell had not come from inside, but from the outside walls of the house—and it was the odor of *gingerbread!*

MY PARENTS WERE MY RIVALS

"Darlings," mom said to my husband Ian and me, "Dad and I would love to have you move into our house with us. It would be good for all of us because you could both go to work—which is what you want—while we take care of the children and be rid of our empty-nest blues."

We were having coffee in the dinette of my parents' big house. From the window we could see the children playing in the backyard. Our ten-year-old, Bess, was swinging her four-year-old sister Sue, while seven-year-old Bob was modeling something in the sandbox. I was barely aware of the children. My mind was churning with too many thoughts and feelings.

I was remembering all the sleepless nights I had spent, sending up voiceless prayers to God for answers to our problems. We were five people crowded in a three-room apartment. Ian's salary could not possibly begin to stretch to meet all our needs. I desperately hoped to be able to return to the work world—but the children were too young.

And now, like a miracle, here seemed to be the answer to my prayers. Within a month we had moved in with my folks. We had our own bedroom; the girls shared one; and Bob loved his cubicle because it was his "very own room".

My folks had lived for thirty-five years in the three-story, Victorian frame house and their mortgage was paid off. They suggested that our share of the expenses go for the children's needs: utilities, food and incidentals based mainly on our own family needs. They took over the taxes, household repairs, etc.

I got a secretarial job that paid well. It made me feel great to be able to dress up and "go out into the world" again. Ian became more relaxed now that our finances were better and living became more comfortable.

We shared the kitchen, garage, bathrooms. And, of course, we shared the children. Our friends envied us. We did not have to pay babysitters, or watch the clock when we went out in the evening. When vacation came around Ian and I had two weeks. We went off by ourselves on a "second honeymoon" to Niagara Falls.

We were having dinner in a lovely restaurant overlooking the falls. I had just made our nightly telephone call home. I had spoken to each member of the family. All was well. I sat staring at my plate, absently swirling my fork into the mashed potatoes. Ian asked, "What's wrong?"

Frowning, I said, "None of the kids asked when we were coming home. No one said they missed us."

"Well, we don't miss anyone either. After all these years of family togetherness it's great just being with you."

I should have been so happy.

The days were idyllic. But each night, after phoning home, I would get that inexplicable "shut out" feeling.

My mind began churning with thoughts I knew were silly, if not downright irrational. Mom was a fabulous cook. Her house always smelled of delicious roasts, fragrant fruits and spices. When the children returned home from school they were assured of a warm hug and a hot, buttery bun on a snowy napkin, or a fresh-baked cinnamon cookie glazed with honey.

I could not blame them for stuffing their mouths. Hadn't I done so as a child? But I recalled that I was always limited by admonitions: "You'll spoil your appetite for supper." Or, "You'll get fat!" There were no restrictions on the grandchildren. They did not forego desserts and they did not get fat. At the end of our vacation, we drove up the driveway. The folks came to the door, hugging us and asking if we had enjoyed ourselves.

"Anything new?" I queried, almost waiting to hear that something had happened. But—everything had gone smoothly.

"The children are in their rooms," Dad said. "I was helping Bob with his penmanship and mom was working with Bess on math."

I was ashamed to discover myself comparing how different it had been when I was young. My folks had owned a restaurant and rarely found the time to study with me. I recalled my feelings of frustration and it horrified me to find my emotions churning. I tried to stifle traitorous thoughts, but they persisted.

I began to suspect that something must be wrong with me, because I was jealous of the love and attention my parents were lavishing on my children.

With the passing days, I felt resentment building up in me. Whenever I returned from work and asked, "What's new?" the children answered, "Nothing." They had already recounted "their day" to mom and dad. Children need instant gratification and the grandfolk were "there" to listen. By the time Ian and I came home everything was anti-climactic.

One evening, at my dressing table I was brushing my hair with savage strokes because I was angry and not sure if I had a reason for that anger. As I regarded my reflection I became aware of how closely I had grown to resemble my mother. Even our voices were so similar that when callers phoned they often mistook one of us for the other. As my lips parted with an "Oh," of surprise, it appeared as though my mother was trying to speak to me.

Of course, the illusion faded quickly and, with it, my black mood dissolved. I became fully aware that this was not some miraculous vision. I had done enough silent communing with God to realize how often that had motivated me to do soul searching.

Now I pondered, "Why did I imagine mom's face in the mirror?" Suddenly, the realization came to me. Silent communication with the Lord is a totally personal experience—but with people there has to be open and frank discussions.

I found mom in the kitchen, just putting dessert into the refrigerator. "Mom," I said, "can you spare a minute for us to talk?" She instantly set everything aside to sit down across the table from me.

"What's the matter, Baby?"

Her old pet name for me brought a rush of loving memories. It helped uncap my feelings.

I heard myself blurting, "You're doing for my children what you didn't do for me. And they can get along fine without us because they've got you." I was horrified at the rush of annoyed words.

I couldn't believe I was really talking like this to my mother. She sat there so quietly that I cried, with remorse, "Oh, mom, I am so ashamed for saying such things to you. You and dad have been super; just super-super and I am an ungrateful beast. No wonder you call me Baby. That's just what I am."

Mother spoke slowly, "You are right. You are our Baby. You will be just that as long as Dad and I are alive. But tell me what do you feel we are doing for the children that we did not do for you?"

"Well—you are so patient with Bess, molding her fingers on the dough for the yeast cookies. You never would even teach me to knead the dough. You said I worked too slowly...."

She nodded. "It's true. You are more methodical than Bess. You think things through until you are sure of every move. That's a compliment to you. It does not make me proud to say that I have no patience to wait for you to learn. It isn't anything lacking in you, but in me."

"In you?" I stared at her in disbelief. "Why would anyone as swift as you slow the pace for me?"

"Well, someone slowed their pace for me long ago." She cocked her head to one side and gently asked, "What else?"

"The toys—buying everything the kids want—everything they don't even need. When I was young you kept saying we could not afford things."

"That was true. We had a hard time making ends meet when you were a child. Your father and I were just building up our business. That's why, now that we can afford to, we give your children as much as we can." She took my hands in hers, "Don't you see, when we give to your children and do for your children, we are really giving and doing for you."

I stared incredulously. Everything suddenly seemed so simple and so clear. Just as my husband and I could not be with our children at all times because of our jobs, so it had been with my parents when I was young. I had never even realized how fortunate it was that they owned the store so I could stay with them. We could not even do that much for our own children today because we had positions that took us out of the home.

Mother continued talking, softly, with understanding: "Why not pretend that the toys we give your children are yours. Make believe that you are still our little girl and that whatever we give our grandchildren we really mean for you to have. That way you can enjoy them two ways—through them and for yourself."

How simply it was said. And how it cleared my feelings and eased my heart. "Oh, mom, I love you." The tenderness bubbled out of me. I walked over and hugged her. "I love you."

"And I love you, too, Baby. I love you very much."

My parents and I were not rivals. We were partners in a golden time together—in the growing-up time of the children and in the greater fulfillment of our own selves.

MARCH OF THE TOYS

The sign above the basement shop read TOY MAKER, Proprietor: Jan Schmidt. It had been blown free of the screws on one side and dangled and swung, creaking, above the boarded-up front.

The burglar gave it hardly a glance as he hurried around the tenement to the back alley. In the 2:00 A.M. darkness, he was well camouflaged in his dark turtle neck and black jeans. At seventeen, Binny was slim and agile. Easily, he leapt up to hook his fingers onto the ladder, pull himself up onto the fire escape and begin trying the windows.

On the first floor, two were secured, but the third was not. Noiselessly, he opened it and slid into the room. His flashlight showed him a nursery. All in pink. Pink rugs, pink Mother Goose wallpaper, pink rocking chair with lace trimmed cushions, pink crib with sleeping baby, pacifier in mouth. The deep carpet cushioned his tread. He moved carefully because the walls were lined high with all manner and sizes of toys and stuffed animals.

He was mystified. The luxurious furnishings were totally unexpected in this run-down neighborhood. But his surprise gave way to anticipation, as he reasoned that if this was only the nursery he would surely find ripe pickings in the rest of the apartment.

He moved into the next room. His flashlight showed him a rather large area which might easily have been the master bedroom. Empty. Totally unfurnished. He moved through the apartment. Living room, bathroom, kitchen. Bare. No furnishings. No signs of habitation.

"This is crazy," he said aloud and jumped because his voice echoed in the vacancy.

On impulse he went to the refrigerator. Unstocked. No formula. No bottles to feed a baby.

He moved back to the bedroom. Standing over the crib he demanded to know, "Who feeds you? Who changes you? Who takes care of you?" The baby slept on.

A sense of foreboding seeped insidiously over Binny. He felt unseen watchers observing him. He spun around. No one was there. Yet he felt the hackles rising on his back. Wrongness. The feeling was growing. His hands felt clammy. His mouth went dry.

Fear was alien to Binny's nature. He had done many jobs with his brother. He was accustomed to the darkness and the stealth and the heightened feeling of anticipation that went with taking chances.

Danger was always a factor in each operation. It was a stimulation to the brothers. The "high" they experienced was akin to that of big game hunters, or deep-sea fishermen, or astronauts who faced their challenges with every nerve alive in their bodies and a soaring sensation of attaining towering reaches beyond the grasp of ordinary men.

He had to think this out. It was not his first burglary job, but always before, he had gone with his nineteen-year old brother, Sealy. Sealy masterminded everything. This time he had decided Binny should venture out on his own. It was Sealy who had chosen this place.

The toymaker owned the building and lived on the first floor. The apartment next to his was for storage of materials for the business. In the two apartments above, lived the toymaker's son and daughter-in-law. In the apartment next door lived the toymaker's older brother, a widower for many years. The son cared for the property since the toymaker had died a few months before.

A strange death. Seated early one morning at his basement workbench Jan Schmidt had lined up twelve iron bowmen which he had recently die cast. No one knows what happened then. An hour later his teen-age apprentice Donny arrived to find his elderly employer slumped over the workbench. Arrows had riddled him and he was dead, with the archers on the table before him, bows in hand but all arrows discharged and none remaining in their quivers. The police investigation said death was caused by a heart attack, but Donny told what he had seen and he and the neighbors knew differently.

Binny and Sealy figured that there would be tools and appliances in the toymaker's apartment, workshop and storage area, so Binny was to case the place and maybe make off with small stuff and report to his brother for a possible later job. But with this disappointing night's find Binny realized he would have to come home empty-handed confessing to a failed mission. He didn't want to disappoint Sealy on his first mission alone.

He mulled over the crib. What if he took the baby? They could ransom her to her uncle. After all the toymaker's son was the heir to the property now. The little girl must be his child. He'd pay good money to get her back.

There was an ominous growl behind Binny. He spun around. A plush lion, perhaps two feet long had detached itself from the mound of toys. It was advancing, tail slowly sweeping from side to side. Binny didn't know whether to laugh or flee. Menaced by a stuffed toy! But the toy opened its mouth, gave forth a sinister roar which showed sharp, dangerous teeth and leapt right for Binny's throat.

The screaming died down and the thing on the floor lay tattered and torn and bleeding, but unmoving.

The door to the next apartment opened. Out came two handmaidens garbed in gray poke bonnets, white bib aprons over shirt waist uniforms with hobble skirts that came below the ankle. They bore pails and brushes and brooms and dust bins. They glided about the room, bagging the body and parts and scouring off blood and gore.

When the scene was immaculate once more, they went to the incinerator, dumped down bag and contents and moved back to the adjacent apartment as though on wheels—which they were.

The superintendent of the housing development was fast asleep beside his wife in their ground floor apartment, but his twenty-one year old son Sealy sat in the dark in the room he shared with his brother Binny. He was growing uneasy. It had been two hours since Binny had left to burglarize the toymaker's house, which was only four blocks away. He should have been back by this time.

Sealy had been burglarizing since he was sixteen and knew that the job he'd sent his kid brother to do held no danger. It would surely net them a couple of hundred in tools and appliances. Sealy never went in for big jobs that would be reported and followed-through by the police. A computer, VCR, cameras, small stuff—easily replaced—would add to his spending money and not endanger him.

His philosophy had certainly seemed to work. He had never been arrested. Living with his parents and working at the local McDonald's, he enjoyed the supplemental income that allowed him to buy luxuries, like his own motorcycle and car. No one suspected that he had not saved up from his salary and from doing odd jobs for the tenants, as his father had taught him.

Sealy was not greedy and he taught Binny, "Lots of tools and appliances can be turned easily into cash. We don't have to reach for expensive jewels, or works of art and get the cops hot on our trail. Works for me."

Indeed it worked fine. They fenced their stuff the very next day after the heist and rarely stored items that could be found in their possession. Sealy gnawed at a nail. So what was taking his kid brother so long. He'd have to go and see.

GOD OF THE MIST

Terrified eyes gleamed out of the darkness of the Parchee's burrow. Kohler with swiftness surprising in a big man, leapt from the igneous path, plunged his hand into the hole, grabbed the small animal by the long ears and dragged it out, paws kicking futility in air.

Parchee meat, he gloated. He turned to his smaller companion, a few paces behind on the narrow rock-path. Start a fire, Ahuila; here's food. He held the animal to eye level enjoying the helpless pawing and the soft panic squeals. After a moment he pulled his stilo-gun from the holster and flicked the button that released the knife. Deliberately he laid the sharp blade to the fur and began to carefully skin the living beast. ZANTHU! The horrified cry brought his knife to a stop. He turned impatiently. Now what, Ahuila?

The boy's soft mouth worked. Slim, like all Venusians, he seemed frailer now for his golden eyes were sick. He pointed to the squealing parchee. "Kill it!" he said, "Do not torment it."

Kohler shrugged his huge shoulders. "You're too squeamish. Get used to the sight of blood," he advised. "There's gonna be lots of it when I become god of your village." His knife resumed his work.

The parchee shrieked in almost human pitch.

"Kill it! Kill it first!" Ahuila was almost sobbing. Then, before Kohler could guess his intentions, he caught the knife handle, plunging the blade into the tortured animal. It died instantly.

Why you yellow Veni! Kohler dropped the parchee and the stilo-gun, caught the boy by the throat and gave a twist. Ahuila went limp. Kohler flung him down. He cursed in a mixture of Venusian and his own Earth tongue and lashed out with a savage foot that sent the prone boy rolling into a shallow dry gully, arms and legs flopping limp. Then he bent to haul the slack weight to him. Ahuila's head lolled back, mouth agape, golden eyes open and sightless.

Kohler looked into the beautiful young face and his mouth twisted with hatred. Dead! He shook the body in bitter rage. He hadn't meant to break his neck. All that fuss about a parchee they were going to cook and eat anyway!

He lifted his eyes to the mountain crest with its wreath of tenuous mist. Somewhere in the peaks up ahead was Ahuila's village. Now he had to find it alone! The Earthman hefted the dead boy to his shoulder and trudged up the volcanic incline, following the natural route that led past jutting porous rocks. He heard the rush of water before a turn gave him sight of a fountain-like geyser. Warm spray splattered him. The sudden sight of the water came as no surprise. The entire way, since their escape from the lowlands prison toward the northern mountains, had been dotted with hot springs and miniature geysers.

Kohler approached as the column started to lose height. He flung the corpse into the spray, watched t being sucked into the receding column and out of sight.

Now let the Earth Police search for a body.

Earth Police! He gave a short laugh of contempt. He could picture them tracking the swamp and jungle lands, thinking that, like all escapees he would make for Hellsport—outlaw territory where the E.P. were powerless. But his plans had changed after they had thrown Ahuila into the same dirty windowless stone cell with him.

What they got you in for? The other had crouched against the wooden-slatted door, hands out, as if crucified. His eyes, big and golden, expressively simple like all Venusians, were fixed on the nearly seven-foot Earthman in awe. It tickled Kohler's vanity—his great size had always been a source of amazement on Venus, where the people were like perfectly formed, beautiful children. And, like children, the deep thunder of his voice created terror or instant obedience in them.

He thundered his question again now. It got results in a stammered flow of a fluid Venusian dialect with which Kohler was totally unfamiliar. But he got the drift.

Bread. Ahuila had stolen some bread. He had thought it would be such an adventure to get out of Vahuhya, to see what lay outside the mountain, but he had not reckoned with the hunger and the dirt and the greed of the town ruled by the Earth uranium monopoly.

Kohler grinned. He verged on saying: "Know what I'm here for? Murder! Killed the foreman. Crushed his head in like an egg—with my bare hands!" He wanted to hold his hands out for the other to see the gnarled, giant fingers with stiff black hairs. He would have liked to see horror grow in those innocent limped eyes and see the boy shrink away as he clenched and unclenched his hands like the claws of a crane. But an innate instinct stopped him and in a moment he was glad he had not spoken, for the boy suddenly prostrated himself at his feet, crying: "ZANTHU, let me go back to the mountains. I will never leave Vayuhya again. I will trim the salt plants from your sacred waters!"

The boy touched slender hand to mouth—salute of Venusians to a god. Kohler stared. It took a while for him to grasp the significance of Ahuila's words and gesture.

Among Venusians worship was a private affair of each district. But the hand to mouth was a universal tribute to godhood. For whatever reason—his giant height or his skin, burnt red-black like the obsidian hills, by the humid winds of the planet—he, Kohler, had been mistaken for the god-incarnate of Ahuila's particular clan.

With some careful conversation, Kohler learned that the boy came from the Volcanic Mountains to the north. This fact was surprising, since most Venusians preferred the low areas near swamps and rivers, where they could give constant moisture to their extremely thirsty skins. Their remote ancestors had been aquatic and natives with webbed digits and gill slits were not unusual, even today.

Vahuhya! The name rolled pleasantly on Kohler's lips. Zanthu, god of Vahuhya!

He had grinned at his first worshipper. "Want to see a little magic to get us out of here?" he said to Ahuila. Wide-eyed, the boy had watched as Kohler shouted for their jailer, a sullen Earthman, who approached with drawn stilo-gun.

"I don't wanna be locked in with no Veni," Kohler had shouted. "Put him in another cell or I'll kill him!"

"Dry up!" the jailer replied.

"Oh yeah! Don't say I didn't warn you!"

He had launched himself upon the unsuspecting Ahuila, making a great pretense of striking him, while the boy babbled mercy of his god. The jailer cursed and unlocked the door. That was what Kohler wanted. He turned, seized the jailer expertly about the throat and squeezed until the man went limp. Then he took the stilo-gun and, motioning the Venusian out of the cell, locked the unconscious man in. In the ever-cloudy murk of the planet's daylight, they crept through the shadows of houses until they got to the underbrush at the edge of the town. From there on, Ahuila took the lead.

But now Ahuila was dead. The way back was closed. His only hope lay in finding Vayuhya. Kohler doggedly continued the torturous climb. Shadows under the darkening sky grew longer. He plodded up, eyes constantly seeking the higher ground. Even his strong corded legs gave under the grueling trek.

He reached a narrow ravine, whose slopes were dotted by weird calcareous cones. He had to twist and squirm his big body between to reach the next rise. Panting he came to the top, resting his head between his arms on the soft rock ground. After a while he lifted his head. And there it was—the Lake of Zanthu!

From the crest where he lay, he could see the lake, like a jewel below him. Red mist hung, fiery, over the water. Clustered on the far side of the bank, were octagonal dwellings of wood with roofs of pastelled sinter taken from the mountainsides that rose in vari-colored terraces to form protecting bowl-sides. With a quick resurgence of strength, Kohler slipped and slid down the crumbling wall of breccia. At the base, just at the edge of the lake, he came to a slithering halt.

For a moment, he thought fatigue had unhinged him. Right ahead was what appeared to be the dark back of a man. After the first amazed moment Kohler realized it was a tall mass of eroded rock, so curiously formed as to look human. He circled the rock and gasped....

Face to face with his own likeness!

Freak volcanic action had carved an image out of obsidian. Zanthu, rock pinnacle, guardian of the Sacred Lake. Amid lesser goblin shapes it towered, with a face beaten into red-black lines by the elements.

Now Kohler understood Ahuila's obeisance. Here was nature's indisputable evidence of Kohler's godship. Turning, he looked across the mists that now hid the small village. Elation made his heart pound. All the cards were running his way. Carefully he knelt at the lakeside feeling the water—warm as body temperature. He stripped the dusty clothes from himself, immersing his long length to wash away the grime. He would come into his godhood cleansed. When he emerged, shaking the droplets away, he looked more carefully at the statue.

The villagers had clothed the loins with a multitude of minute leaves of the salt plants that abounded in the lake shallows. The painstaking task of twining the small stems into a garment took Kohler's thick fingers many hours, yet he never lost patience.

At last it was done. He was clothed like his counterpart. He circled the lake, mists beading him with fine moisture. At the further end, he became aware of thin, high singing.

As he drew near, the outlines of a structure grew out of the mist. It was largest of all the dwellings he had glimpsed from the ridge. Several window-like openings were covered by filmy material which blew out with the wind, so that he could see a congregation of people inside. Theirs were the high sweet voices raised in a singing prayer. He could not catch the words, but the oft-repeated name of Zanthu made him realize he had come in the midst of their services.

Good! He could not have timed it better.

He peered into the circular room. There was a crude raised dais—apparently an altar—upon which was carved a crude figure, roughly resembling the great statue of Zanthu.

He strode toward the altar and they scattered to either side of him. The smell of the offering was tantalizing.

"I, Zanthu, accept your offer!" His great voice filled the room. The villagers murmured and fell flat before him too awed to lift their eyes. The little priestess sank to her knees covering her face. Only the priest stood erect. His mouth worked for a minute before the words came out so low that only Kohler could hear.

"Who are you?"

Kohler's eyes narrowed. "ZANTHU," he answered.

The priest shook his head. "You do not talk like our clan."

Speech. The Earthman had not figured on this, that his accent was different, that he was unfamiliar with the dialect. He determined to bluff it out.

"Do you question your god?"

The congregation quivered as under a storm. But the priest stood his ground.

"I do not know who you are, but you are no god!"

Black rage swept over Kohler. Godhood within his reach, food to fill his empty belly and Venusian women his for the taking and this fool of a priest challenged it.

"Die, false priest!" he cried. "Die by the magic of Zanthu!" He pulled the stilo-gun from its concealment in his loin cloth and beamed the priest cleanly through the head. Without a word the Venusian toppled dead before him.

There was a horror-stricken gasp, then the congregation bolted for the door, pushing and milling. The little priestess bent to the dead priest. She touched him, then straightened, shuddering and would have fled after the others, but the Earthman's great black-haired hand circled her wrist like steel.

"Not you," he said. "You are dedicated to your god." And he laughed softly.

Thus did Kohler take up residence in the shrine of Zanthu. Luala the priestess became his trembling slave, messenger between himself and the people. He declared the shrine inviolate, so that none dared approach. The body of the priest he himself cast into the Sacred Lake waters. Then he commanded his people to fashion a bell by which he might summon them to his worship.

Every day he asked: "When will the bell be ready, Luala?" Her full red mouth quivered when she answered: "They are working fast. I will tell them to hurry more." And she would run on bare brown feet out the door.

In the open square around which the houses clustered, the first of the bell forges burned. Usually the women gathered here to do their weaving and plaiting of garments, to tell their simple bits of gossip; the men to do their simple bartering of the crops of the individual fields or ornamental stones worked out of hardened breccia from the hills. But now they went out in two streams of workers—those who dug into the terraced slopes for copper and those who worked the fires making the burnished metal pliable.

Progress was slow. Kohler grew hard with impatience.

He ordered Luala: "Tell them if they don't get finished by tomorrow I will call fire out of the earth to burn them at their forges." She paled and ran to exhort her people to greater speed.

There was no sleep in Vahuhya that night. Even the women took turns at the fires. But with the deadline close they seemed far from the goal. "Zanthu," Luala begged, "have mercy on them. They cannot finish in time. Please do not call the fire upon them."

He laughed into her pallid face.

He stayed at the doorway long hours, watching the never-dying forge fires and the sweat-streaked groups working in terror to avert his wrath. With dawn the little priestess grew babbling in her fear for her people. "Zanthu! Kind and gracious god, give them more time. Visit me with your anger, but do not burn the village."

For a while he enjoyed her fear. After a while the endless pleas began to grate against his ears. He kicked at her savagely. She shrank back for the moment, was silent for the moment and then crept near, begging again. "SHUT UP!" he shouted and gave her a swift cuff over the mouth. She coughed blood from a bitten tongue. Her great golden eyes raised again in appeal. "Mercy!" It was like a croak.

In a fury he lifted her by the shoulders, slapped her with his open hand—one cheek, the other, back and forth, back and forth—and her head rocked under the blows until her body sagged and her eyes closed. But the rage was upon him. He battered her, head and body, open fist and closed, until his hands were red with her blood.

After a while he stopped, looked at the limp thing he held—the blackened tongue, the toothless mouth, the swollen face. There was breath in her yet, but all beauty was gone. The sight disgusted him. He pulled out his stilo-gun, placed it at her temple and fired.

No one saw him leave the shrine. No one saw him fling the dead priestess into the mists, into the sacred red lake. But when he returned he saw the villagers marching toward him, chanting his name, merry children, their task complete—the bell was finished.

He raised his hands, palms out. They stopped, waiting uneasily. He let them wait, deliberately. In the stillness no one moved. Then he spoke, his voice carrying over them, rebounding from the hillsides: "Luala, your priestess has given herself to the spirit of the bell so that you might finish in time. For that she will live forever and her voice will speak to you in the toll of the bell. But now"—his eyes swept from woman to woman, "I will choose a new priestess. Send to me your maidens that I might give honor to one."

Deliberately he moved back into the doorway of the shrine, to wait at the altar for the flower of their women.

His days passed idyllically. Seritah, the new priestess, was more beautiful than Luala, even younger. The villagers had fashioned for him a couch of beaten iridescent metal they had mined from the pitted slopes. They had cushioned it with soft baya leaves draped over with yardage of filmy material. They brought him offerings of food and ornaments of firestone and micalite, the two most precious stones of Venus. And, however they clothed him, he ordered that they likewise ornament the obsidian statue.

For a while he was content to lie on his couch letting Serita feed to him the sacrificial foods, or cleanse his body with the warm waters from his sacred Lake. He amused himself by speaking to her in his native Earth tongue, a language she did not understand and therefore took to be divine. He recounted the adventures he had had, the places he had been. When he recalled some particular deed he would roar with sudden laughter that sent her shrinking back in terror.

"This being a god isn't so bad," he said one day to her uncomprehending ears. "But back on Earth the gods had a little more excitement than you ever have up here. Not just singing and bowing to the floor. Why, they had special festivals, dancing and singing, big bonfires. Lots of hooting and hollering. Gave it a little color."

He reached out, pulled the blue mancha flowers out her hair, so that it came cascading down to her bare shoulders. He ran his fingers through the silken pile, twining and tugging it as he talked: "Why I remember reading history about this group of Mayans. Made sacrifices to the sun-god. Had living victims. And cut out their hearts."

His own words rang in his ears. Kohler grew silent. His fingers gave a convulsive clench that pulled a great fistful of the golden hair. Seritah gave a scream of pain. But Kohler did not hear. His eyes were brooding on the altar and the sacred water that bathed the little replica of Zanthu. Seritah continued to whimper until it penetrated his concentration. He turned burning eyes to her. Her head was at an angle from the tautness of his pull. He did not release his cruel grip. Instead, he pulled tighter so that her head came back, all the way and he could stare into her pain-filled eyes.

"Know what?" he etched the words. "I'm going to put some life into this godhood. Gonna have a festival. Gonna do it right like I read in books." He released her with a suddenness that sent her reeling. "We're gonna have hootin' and hollerin'; dancin' and drinkin'. And know what else? I'm gonna pick me a bevy of priestesses and really set up a heaven."

He decreed the time of the festival: the time of the harvest of the Tuva fruits. Tuva, the main crop of Vahuhya, grew juicy and golden, large as a man's head. From the fresh fruits the Tuva drink was made. The pit contained a sweet nut that was used as a confection. The silken fibers that grew around the fruit were carefully combed and spun into material. Tuna harvest was a time for rejoicing. What more fitting time to claim as sacred to a god.

He commanded the women to deck themselves in flower garments and the men to build an altar of stone beside his statue. The best fruits of the harvest were to be tribute to him. He himself fashioned the drums made of wood and the tanned hide of the parchee. And he taught some of the young men to beat a savage tattoo that would stir the blood.

He coached Seritah on how to lead the procession that was to wend its way from the village to the newly erected altar. He himself would officiate as his own high priest.

The day dawned with the usual pall of the planet's days. Ever present clouds hung low over the surrounding peaks and the red mists of the lake seemed, if anything, angrier. For hours the villagers carried their plaited baskets of perfect Tuvas to the altar. The perfume of the pink-tinted fruits made the air rich, like wine.

To each donor of fruit Kohler gave a large quaff of the Tuva drink. It amazed him that it only brought a flush to their skins, but did not fill them with the headiness he himself experienced.

At his signal, the women came forward—a flowerlike procession—in their mancha costumes. They came singing, as Kohler had commanded and Seritah led them to the foot of the altar. Slowly the drums began to beat, adding a throbbing note to the singing. For a moment the women's voices faltered. Kohler frowned. Seritah made a convulsive movement and the singing went on, but it held a troubled note as though the women hesitated.

What was the matter with them anyway! Kohler lifted his hands and began a meaningless chant which was signal for the men to come dancing out of the village to surround the women. He meant this to be a love orgy as he imagined was given to pagan Earth gods. But when the men finally did get the signal, they came with a bewildered shuffling that caused the women to stop singing altogether.

Glaring down from his altar of stone, Kohler chanted his gibberish in a more thunderous voice.

That only caused his congregation to mill around fearfully, completely at a loss as to how to obey him. Even the drummers he had so carefully taught faltered, adding an uncertain tempo to what he had meant to be compulsive. With a snort of disgust he came down from the high place.

He would show them himself! He came to the foremost of the young men. "DANCE!" he shouted.

The youth made a few fumbling motions of obedience. This was not inspirational! Kohler caught his arm, flinging him back and forth violently. "DANCE HARD!"

Instead the boy, as soon as he was released, fell at Kohler's feet. Incensed, the big man lashed out with a suddenness that caught the youth flush, smashing his jaw.

The crowd moaned. But Kohler ignored the mutilated youth. He turned to the next man in line, pointing imperiously to the woman beside him. "Take her!"

The man only stared.

In a fury the Earthman reached out, pulled the flowered garment from the woman. "All of you!" he roared at the men, "That's what you must do!"

They shrank from him, every eye mirroring disbelief. He seized another woman, tore off her garments, then another. Suddenly the ranks of women broke. They scattered, high voiced, crying. He was left with the mancha blossoms in his hands. Savagely he flung the man down, seized the man nearest to him and lifting him by hips and neck, brought him down like a Tuva stalk, over his knees, breaking his back.

He reached. But there was no one in his reach. As far as he could see, his congregation was fleeing. Roaring, he pursued, but their small bodies were lithe, their feet swift as geysers. In a moment, they were gone, up over the terraced slopes, among the boulders, beyond the peak rim.

Kohler shouted, ran. Wherever he saw a movement he made for it, killing lust upon him. But it was only the nodding of the mancha flowers, the rustle of the salt plants. He was a god without worshippers—alone with an altar of stone and a statue of obsidian.

Leave him, would they? He would show them!

He pounded along the silent, red-misted lake. Back to the village—an avenging god. From house to house he went, each one open and desolate. And when he emerged each house carried a hungry hot core of flame that ate at the materials, licked at the walls, blackened the floors. He came to the last house at the edge of the village. And then he looked back. Fire was dancing a sacrificial rite to the tune of his violent heart.

Disobey him, would they? Let them come sneaking back in the night. Everything they had would be gone, consumed in the bonfire of Zanthu's festal day. He stood at the edge of the lake, laughing with the irony of his joke. Over the roar of the flames and his own laughter, he did not hear *them* approach. They shouted over and over again, until he heard,

"*Don't move, Kohler!*"

Laughter froze on his lips. Slowly he turned. Coming to him with drawn stilo-guns were a dozen uniformed men. The Earth Police!

"No!" he screamed. "You can't be here! You're looking for me in the jungles!" He closed his eyes to shut them out. Their leader's tone was wry. "Not the jungles—thanks to your message."

Kohler's eyes flew open. His lips framed the question! *"Message?"*

The leader held up something. In the red fire glow at his back, Kohler saw the skull with the stilo-hole bored in it.

"This came out in our reservoir, fed from the mountain springs. We received two of them. One's a woman's. Venusians don't own stilo-guns. But we might have searched the whole mountain without success if you hadn't sent up your fire-signal." He pointed to the smoking, burning red village.

Kohler's face writhed. If he had not been such a big man, he might have cried.

Suddenly he turned to make a break. But before he moved a dozen paces, their weapons spoke. The impact of the bullets turned his giant body like a twister. Momentum carried him back toward the very edge of his sacred lake.

The last human words he heard were: "We'll pick up your bones in the reservoir at Earth camp, Kohler!" Then he toppled into the waiting water. The red mists swirled madly, then closed—quiescent—as though nothing had passed through, nothing at all.

THE BIRD AND THE THREE WISE MEN

Through the deep foliage of the forest the bird could see the Star. Shining brilliantly in the dark sky, it was like a beacon in the heavens. Spreading his small wings, he fluttered up, following the silver light.

A watch fire down below caught his attention and he flew for a closer look. It was an encampment of emerald tents, encircling the fire.

The tall, handsome leader, garbed in green with sequins that sparkled where firelight touched, came forward and courteously greeted the bird.

"Do you also follow the Star?" he asked. And the bird said yes.

"We, too. And you are welcome to join us."

"Thank you," answered the bird, "but I will follow the Star, wherever it leads me." And off he flew.

He came upon an encampment of crimson tents, circled about a watch fire. The sentries were portly, muscular men, garbed in crimson with stripes of gold that reflected in the firelight. The leader, a giant of a man, was bare-chested. A tunic, bound at his throat, swirled to his hips.

He said to the bird, "I see you fly with a purpose. Do you, perhaps, follow the Star?"

"I do," the bird replied.

"You are welcome to join us for we also go that way." The bird thanked him, but said he would continue alone. And on he went. Flying through the night, his attention was again caught by the blaze of firelight.

Down he swooped to see this new encampment. The company was resplendent in princely attire of gold weskits and fitted tights. They wove in a circle, clasping hands. They caroled in voices of most melodious harmony, yet never broke the pattern of moving in line with the Star.

"Sir Bird," a spokesman of the group called out, "Come and sing and dance with us. Surely you must have a most appealing voice. It will certainly enhance our group."

"I thank you. Your faith is flattering. Another night, perhaps, I will find time to sing with you, but now there is a Star to follow and a mission to fulfill."

The Star never faltered in the course that ran true. And the shepherds with their flocks and the kings on their jewel-bedecked camels realized that wondrous deeds were about on this night.

The roads were packed with wayfarers who traveled to have their names listed in a census. In a town called Bethlehem, a husband and wife and a newborn baby boy could find no lodging. The innkeeper advised them to place the child's cradle in the manger in the stable. In the heavens the Star hung above the stable, its brilliance lighting the night.

The Emerald King and his followers filed into the stable. The babe was crying. The breasts of Mary, the young mother, had not yet filled with milk.

The Emerald King and courtiers began to carol and to dance to make the child happy. But the child was hungry and cried. The Wise Men in their crimson array wrestled and grappled and flung each other to the mat.

The child continued to cry.

The Wise Men in their golden raiment offered gifts of gold, frankincense and myrrh. But the babe continued to cry.

The small plain bird knew why he had followed the Star and why, perched on the manger, it sang to a crying baby. The song of the bird was so exquisite that the babe forgot his hunger and grew quiet in his mother's arms.

And better than the gifts of the Three Wise Kings to the child, was the glorious song of a plain little bird called the Nightingale.

BACKYARD ALLEY CAT QUEEN

Christmas!

The air was filled with the frenzy of human activities. But all it meant to the stray cats was the necessity of getting out of the path of some large boot, or being impatiently shooed away.

Cat Cat, a gray-and-white-striped alley cat, was little different from others of her breed. She was a good hunter, having lived her one year of life roaming the empty lots and back alleys of the tenements.

Cat Cat had been fending for herself for such a long time she had rare memories of her beginnings. But there were flashes of those early times when she had lived with humans in a house that was warm and a mom cat who had sweet milk and a ready tongue to clean her babies.

There had been only one harsh voice: "It's enough, with litter after litter. Cat and kittens have to go. This place stinks all the time."

A child of the house caught Cat Cat up in her arms, fleeing to the yard. Cardboard boxes were plentiful. She bedded Cat Cat on the cardboard and newspaper. In the shelter of an overhang, the cat could be protected from the elements.

Every day before her father would come home, the child would come out with a bowl and pour her school container of milk for Cat Cat. When she could scrape some leftover meat, the cat would have an extra treat.

However, one day, it came to an end. The child and her family moved out of the neighborhood. That was when Cat Cat's instincts helped her to survive.

There were mice in the tenement. Not only did they offer sport, but fresh food. Cat Cat soon learned to be a most agile mouser.

Then trouble came in the form of a harsh winter. Cat Cat hated the cold. The snow fell and blanketed her cardboard boxes and soaked the old newspapers. Cat Cat's world had turned frigid and when she walked, her feet sank in snow and filled her paw pads with ice.

One day, the heavy tenement door leading to the back yard did not close because of the accumulation of snow. Cat Cat slipped in and was instantly enveloped in the steam-heated warmth of the building.

She would have stopped to lick the melting ice particles off her fur, but a familiar movement caught her eye.

A mouse!

She did not stop for her usual game of toying with the creature. She had been too long without food. In quick time, she dispatched the mouse. She polished it off, leaving no evidence of its demise.

Then, another gray form came fleeing past. Again, Cat Cat pounced. But this time, not being as famished as she had been with the first, she ate more delicately, leaving evidence of her prey.

At that moment, the superintendent of the complex came down the hall.

"A cat!" he exclaimed. "How did you get in?"

He was on the verge of chasing Cat Cat out the door when he saw the mouse remains. He was so astonished that he could only stop and stare. Finally, he declared "By golly, a first-class mouser!"

He held out his hand. Warily, Cat Cat eyed him. But he bent and began to pat her head.

"Good cat," he praised. "Good Cat Cat."

When she allowed him to scratch her head, he was even more lavish with his praise.

"You're a good girl, a real good girl."

Sensing that he meant her no harm, she permitted him to lift her up and continue to pet and praise her.

"This place needs a cat like you. Won't my little girl be pleased! She keeps asking for a pet for Christmas. You can be her Christmas cat—and also work for me." He chuckled. "My partner, the mouser."

Still chuckling, he went back into his apartment with Cat Cat in his arms. As his wife looked astonished, his six-year old daughter ran forward in delight.

"Here's the Christmas present you wanted," her father told her, putting Cat Cat into her arms. "Your present arrived a day early, but this is one present that couldn't be wrapped and put under the tree."

The little girl cuddled the cat, kissing her and kissing her. Her mother said, "Your cat needs to be towel-dried. We may like snow for Christmas, but cats don't."

While mom dried Cat Cat, Father took one of the small cartons form the basement and made a litter box. He drove to the store to buy kitty litter, cat toys and other necessities.

When he came back, he was all smiles.

"Daddy, what did you buy? What did you buy?" His daughter tugged, trying to see what the packages held.

Out came a plastic litter box and a bag of litter. When it was ready, he set the litter box in a corner under the two-legged sink. Then he showed Cat Cat, one paw at a time, how to sift through the litter. She mastered that quickly. As a reward, he took a small Santa Claus hat and put it on Cat Cat, pulling the pom-pom rakishly sideways.

Next, the father took sprigs of mistletoe and hung them from light fixtures in the ceiling. He unwrapped a satin cat pillow and placed Cat Cat upon it, underneath the mistletoe.

"You get kissed if you're under the mistletoe."

Cat Cat curled up on her satin pillow and purred. She had finally discovered what all the fuss was about Christmas.

Christmas was all about love.

978-0-595-48051-7
0-595-48051-9